A QUESTION OF VIRTUE

Carolyn Davidson

A KISMET™ Romance

METEOR PUBLISHING CORPORATION
Bensalem, Pennsylvania

To Nancy, Pam, and Tanya,
for their encouragement
and to Mr. Ed—who loves me.

CAROLYN DAVIDSON

Marriage to her high school sweetheart, caring for their six children and working full time occupied most of Carolyn Davidson's hours up until six years ago. After she and her husband deserted Michigan for the sunny south, she found the time to realize her lifelong ambition and began writing about her favorite subject—romance.

ONE

"I really don't feel like going to a party, Marcie." Softly spoken, the words fell between the two women and a wheedling smile appeared on Marcie's lips. Her hands were busy with the ritual of cosmetics, which required at least thirty minutes every time she walked out the door of her apartment. She concentrated on her eyes, wide-open and brilliant, lashes heavy with three applications of mascara, as she surveyed herself in the mirror.

"Ummm . . . you'll love it, sweetie." She flicked a glance at the face that was in shadow behind her, faintly blurry in the mirror. Green eyes met hers and an oval face surrounded by a cloud of dark, curly hair moved closer.

"Marcie! It isn't my kind of party." Her voice was firmer and she crossed her arms over her breasts as she settled back for battle.

The slender blond turned from the mirror and surveyed her guest's belligerent stance. "You haven't been to a party since the beer brawl on graduation night in Goose Creek, sugar." She grinned and for a moment, her companion caught a glimpse of the close friend she hadn't seen in four years. Then the facade of elegant boredom slid back into place and the eyes that returned to the mirror contained a shadow of pain.

What am I doing here, Sara thought. Not for the first time, the question raced through her mind. Marcie Wright, high-school cheerleader, fellow conspirator in childhood pranks, confidante extrordinaire, her best friend . . . had changed. Drastically. Green eyes swept over the satin dress that clung to every curve. Marcie hadn't lost her figure, that was for sure. The shoes, if they could be called that, had impossibly high heels—stiletto heels—that had to be awfully hard to walk on, she thought. Marcie's hair had been bleached and teased into a cloud of off-white brilliance. Her nails were another sort of brilliant, long and shiny with three coats of polish that hovered just short of purple.

Again, her head shook in bewilderment and she sighed, a whisper that sounded like acquiescence to Marcie.

"You won't be sorry." She spun to grasp Sara's slender, ringless fingers. Sara stood open-mouthed, stunned by the glittering vision before her. The mirror hadn't done Marcie justice. She was polished, posed as if for the camera, and Sara recognized what she privately called "Marcie's model look." Not a success yet, Marcie was still doing catalogues on good days, working in dingy little studios for disreputable looking little men the rest of the time, earning barely enough to sustain body, let alone soul, yet determined to get to the top.

To the small-town eyes of Sara, she was big-city stuff, glamorous, exciting, all of that. And without a trace of envy, she decided that the price Marcie paid for her life was costly. She sacrificed too much to maintain her small but glossy apartment; her wardrobe, carefully chosen to enhance her seductive beauty, the hectic rush of a schedule that included parties and late nights, all were foreign to Sara. All were viewed with doubtful green eyes that settled now on the finished product.

"Please, Marcie. Take no for an answer, will you." Sara carefully stepped back and the hands that bore a ring on almost every finger flashed a gesture of aggravation as Marcie shook her head.

"Sara! I'll be right beside you. No one will bother you and some really important people are going to be there." She smiled, a secret smile that promised much. "A man I know . . ." The smile widened and she shrugged, dismissing the thought in favor of another. "On top of that, the food is being catered and we haven't had a decent meal today."

Her mouth twitched and then she grinned appealingly as she coaxed her friend with an arm about her slender waist. Sara lifted her chin, her gaze questioning and what she saw tipped the scales. Marcie's blue eyes were sincere. She really wanted Sara to have a good time on this vacation and so far her week had been spent with a guidebook in one hand and a subway directory in the other.

Not that Sara had complained, but to Marcie's way of thinking there were better things to do in New York than look at statues and churches. Museums were even more boring and absolutely no one went to Ellis Island. But Sara had done all of that and more. Surely, it was time for a little fun. Her smile coaxed Sara's weakening defense and finally, with a shrug, she gave in.

"All right, I'll go with you. But don't blame me if I embarrass you or act like a small-town girl." She ran her hands down the sides of a sea-green dress, the only thing she had brought with her suitable for a party. The lines were simple, clinging to her small, high breasts, just a suggestion of cleavage in the vee of the neckline, and then shaping to her hips, which were rounded softly and firmly. A golden chain tied loosely at her waistline suggested the trimness of her body and another gold chain around her neck ended in a locket. If she had known how masculine eyes were drawn to that spot, she would have never worn it.

But Sara was unaccustomed to being viewed by strange men and the looks of passersby during her week in the city had not penetrated her total concentration on sightseeing. Sightseeing was what she had come for. The male half of the population was not essential in her life. She found it easy to ignore them, simple to look past them or through them, safer to keep herself aloof from men in general.

Safe. Would she be safe with Marcie? Would she really stick with her tonight? Sara looked in the bathroom mirror; Marcie behind her, positions reversed. Her earrings were simple, golden chains that fell almost an inch below her earlobe. She pulled her hair back and wound it quickly into a loose arrangement that hugged her nape, sliding pins into place with the ease of long practice.

"Why don't you leave it loose? Men love long hair." Marcie's reasoning was typical of her longstanding theory. Do what men expect. Dress to attract them. Use and discard.

"I only leave it down at home." Her fingers were quick, only a few curling strands escaped the pins and hung in careless abandon, enhancing the purity of her profile.

Marcie sobered. "I'd forgotten how beautiful you are, Sara. No one will even look at me with you around."

She was almost serious, Sara thought. And then, with a flashing smile, that idea was doused as Marcie turned away, her eyes sparkling, hands flashing as the light caught the sparkling rings she wore. She looked the part. Model, popular girl-about-town, her speech modified until the soft accent she had carried from South Carolina four years ago had all but disappeared.

"I've missed you, Marcie." The blond head turned and eyes met. For a moment, the perfectly constructed face softened and Sara saw a glimpse again of her childhood friend. Then, a brilliant smile lit the generous mouth and Marcie tugged at her.

"I've missed you, too, sweetie, but if we don't hurry, all the shrimp will be gone and I'm starved."

She picked up her purse and slung the narrow strap over her shoulder, lifting the flap to check for her keys. Another quick look in the mirror assured her that the lacquer was holding, her hair was perfect. She preened just a bit. She really had nothing to fear from Sara— the classic lines of her dress, the subdued makeup, her unfashionable hairdo, all served to label her. Perhaps tonight would draw her from her shell, maybe she would attract enough attention to encourage her to leave South Carolina behind and make a fresh start. Heaven knows, she could use one.

"I don't feel like another party, Jeff!" His palms rested on denim-covered hips and his expression was grim. Enough was enough, thought Callen Emerson Hyatt. Florida was looking better by the minute. Jeff had dragged him to three parties in one week and tonight was the final straw.

"There's a gal coming to this one that I want you to meet, Cal." His chin was an object of close scrutiny, the razor sliding carefully through a layer of foam as

Jeff Walker shaved for the second time since six that morning. Darn his heavy beard . . . women liked a smooth approach, he had discovered through the years and that did not include bristles against tender skin.

He rinsed his face with warm water and raised his head, dripping into the sink as he viewed his jaw. A quick rubdown with the towel that hung around his neck, followed by a splash of after-shave, completed his ablutions and he turned to face his friend.

Leaning on the door jamb across his bedroom stood the man who had fought beside him in the final days of Vietnam, where a bond had been forged that knit two men together regardless of the distance that separated them through the years.

Cal, tall, confident in his strength, blond, and tanned from the Florida sun that shone on him year-round as he worked his cattle ranch. Cal, who had kept him alive more than once, who had brought him back from an insane world where no one could be trusted, where life was cheap and death was sometimes welcomed by those who could not face the reality of living in the hell that was southeast Asia. But they had survived and again, as he had more times than he could count, Jeff silently thanked the friend who leaned so casually in the doorway before him.

"A girl, Jeff?" His grin was knowing. "I outgrew girls a long time ago. An occasional woman, maybe. But girls are not my speed." He straightened and the hand that had rested easily on his hip slid into his back pocket. "Okay. But this is it. Tomorrow night we watch the Mets play ball on television and I rest up for the trip home. Agreed?"

Hands waved in the air as Jeff laughed heartily. "Whatever you say. I just don't want to miss this one. I've been trying to make time with Marcie Wright for weeks and she's been tied up with a jerk from Queens who promised her a shot at a modeling job in the Caribbean. The guy was trying to juggle two gals at the same time and when Marcie found out that he had scored with her rival, she backed out of the deal.'' He lifted an eyebrow. ''She's no saint, but she's not cheap. She sure isn't into selling herself.'' A pale-blue shirt slid into place and he buttoned the bottom four buttons, tucking the tails into his slacks with deft motions and rolling up the sleeves twice.

''Do they? Sell themselves . . . literally?'' Cal's eyes were veiled, but Jeff sensed the scorn behind the words.

He shrugged and bent to smooth his hair back with the brush that lay on his dresser, looking into the mirror that was hung just a bit too low over the chest of drawers.

''Some do. Maybe not for money, but for a big opportunity.'' He looked in the mirror and met the dark eyes that glittered with disgust. ''Hey, this is the big city, Cal. Not that I think Marcie is for sale.'' With a grin, he turned and his lower lip jutted a bit. ''But with a little coaxing and a few dates under my belt, I might get a taste of magnolias. It's worth a try, anyway. Wait till you see her. Tall, a little slim but models usually are. Blond and classy.''

Probably just what I need, thought Callen Hyatt. A long night in the big city. Maybe her girlfriend, this girl he was supposed to meet, would be ready and willing to charm him. After months of branding cattle, culling and selling off his extra stock, rebuilding fences and building a new stock barn, he was ready for some relaxation. The problem was that the women who had been available at the other parties this week hadn't appealed to him. Not that he could afford to be fussy; in his cowboy boots and Levis, he presented a less-than-cosmopolitan picture.

As if reading his mind, Jeff sorted through the closet and tossed a pair of light colored slacks at him. "Tonight I want you to get out of those jeans and put on a pair of real pants. Here, these will do." He pulled a shirt from the several that Cal had brought with him. The chocolate stripe against a lighter brown background blended with the slacks he had chosen, and he watched as Cal gave in.

"Okay, tonight we meet society, all dressed up." He smiled and the flash of his teeth against the golden tan caused Jeff to pause thoughtfully.

"Just remember, Marcie is mine. The girlfriend is fair game. The rest of the female population is all yours." He was prepared to be generous. "Let's go, Cal. I'm hungry and Mark told me that Carol's caterers specialize in shrimp."

The music was loud, the apartment was crowded, and the buffet table was surrounded by laughing guests, all of whom seemed to know each other. From his vantage point, next to the door that led into the hallway, Cal viewed the assortment of humanity with jaded eyes. The usual group. Women looking for a man to latch onto. Men looking for a woman to fill the lonely hours till morning.

He shook his head. New York really wasn't so different from anywhere else, he supposed. Just different people, all alike underneath the outer wrappings. Here it was silk and satin and glittering gold. Chunky bracelets, heavy earrings that swung as heads turned, eyes looking for new faces. Women, alike the world over; looking, taking, grasping, then moving on to another chump. He amused himself for a moment as he watched Jeff making time with the elusive Marcie.

Her hair, silvery and spiked in the latest style, her eyes fashionably darkened and emphasized, her mouth curving in a warm smile that was obviously dazzling Jeff—she was something to behold. Jeff had labeled her. She was classy, all right. But apparently she had left her girlfriend at home. No mirror image hung in her shadows. In fact, since Jeff had approached her thirty minutes ago, she had faithfully directed her attention toward him and they had managed to create a space of their own in the crowded room.

Probably just as well. She definitely wasn't his type. The girlfriend must have changed her mind, thank goodness. He was off the hook. In fact, as soon as he managed to get a plate full of that food, he planned on heading for the front door and making a quick getaway. From the looks of Jeff and Marcie, neither of them would miss him.

"What I wouldn't give to be home right now." The words were loud in the small powder room and Sara leaned against the door, her eyes closed. It was no use, she might as well go back to the party and try again to get near the buffet table. Somehow it hadn't seemed worth it the first time. The crowd wasn't rude, just thoughtless, interested in their loud conversations, calling greetings over her head, and ignoring her attempts to casually ease her way toward the food. The rumble of her stomach was the prompting she needed, and with renewed determination she opened the door and slipped into the dimly lit hallway.

The door into the large room where the party was underway was partially blocked by a body. The man who stood with his back to her presented an obstacle she wasn't about to squeeze passed. His wide shoulders in the brown shirt were formidable. Her eyes slid to the trim waist and down the narrow hips to the long legs that were braced against the doorway. One hand hung casually, thumb tucked into his side pocket, and she saw the fingers flex as he drew them into his palm. The fist knuckled into his hip and her eyes rested on the muscles that flexed in his forearm, where light whorls of hair curled under the rolled-up sleeve of his shirt.

Her slender hand reached out to touch him and her fingers retreated as they brushed the golden curls on his arm. A faint tingle at the warmth of his tanned skin rocketed up her arm and turned to a scalding sensation that startled her as he turned quickly at her tentative touch.

"Excuse me, please?" A small woman stood in the hallway, waiting for him to move so she could pass into the scene of action. She looked at him for a moment and he caught an impression of green eyes that met and then nervously skittered away from his. Her hair was wispy around her face, caught up in a . . . his eyes narrowed. His mother would have called it a bun, he supposed. A rather artful arrangement, really; twisted against the nape of her neck.

He stepped to one side and watched her as she passed him. The gentle sway of her hips drew his eyes. Then his gaze slid down to focus on her slender, shapely legs that moved hesitantly toward the table where the food beckoned enticingly. Long legs for a small girl, he decided after his second look. It was time to change his vantage point. His glance at the front view had been quick. A glimpse of green eyes, an averted face, a dimple, he tried to remember . . . no use. He would have to take action.

With unhurried motions, he advanced toward her and watched as she hesitated. The crowd around the table had thinned out and she finally made her way to the end where a pile of plates designated the starting place.

Sara picked up the china plate and smiled. Parties in Goose Creek featured Chinet and plastic forks. Her friends there would hoot in disbelief at the array of foods that tempted her here. Paté, caviar. It looked terrible, she thought. Small open-faced sandwiches with strange toppings. A lot of green stuff to sort through. Raw vegetables must be popular everywhere. The bowl of promised shrimp was in the center of the table and she reached for the tongs to serve herself.

"Leave a few for me." The low voice in her ear startled her and the tongs clicked together as she dropped the pinkish-orange specimen she had lifted from the bowl. Her eyes looked over her shoulder in surprise and met the chest of Mr. Brown Shirt. The golden hair that filled the vee of his partially unbuttoned shirt met her gaze and she swallowed hard. There should be a law against men who crept up on women, she thought. Her eyes moved carefully up, past his chin, past his mouth—corners tilted just a little— skimmed his nose, and then she caught her breath as she met the amused gaze of the owner of the brown shirt and curly-haired chest.

"Didn't mean to startle you, green eyes." The rest of her face was a pleasant surprise. A short, straight nose above lips that were full and unadorned with lipstick. Pink cheeks that owed their color to her embarrassment instead of artificial blush. A round chin that held a very small dimple, matched by larger ones that nestled on either side of her mouth as a grin tugged at the lips that opened to show white teeth with just a tiny gap in the center.

"That's all right. I was just trying to get the biggest shrimp." She whispered in a low voice, "I didn't eat dinner before we came." With fingers that betrayed her loss of assurance by trembling on the tongs, she once more reached toward the bowl.

"Here, let me." He slipped his hand past her and took the serving utensil, his arm warm against her ribs as he lifted several shrimp at a time and piled them on her plate.

"Oh, that's more than enough." Her protest was quick, but he ignored it as he reached for the bowl again. The sauce was in a silver dish and the ladle seemed tiny in his hand as he measured out a pool of it onto one side of the seafood on her plate. The sharp odor of horseradish bit at her nose and she turned her head and breathed deeply, inhaling a scent from his body as he pressed against her that caused a shiver to begin at the nape of her neck. A bit spicy with maybe a touch of lemon. She couldn't place it, but it filled her senses and she became aware of the length of him as he leaned over her, his chest touching her shoulder and the back of her head, his long legs leaning into hers.

"This is for both of us. No sense in dirtying two plates." His explanation was simple and he guided her down the length of the table, piling crackers, cheese, and a brownish spread that smelled a bit like garlic and onion in an arrangement that finally threatened to overflow the edges.

"That should do us for a little while," he stated with finality. His hand was firm under her elbow as he steered her away from the table and out an open door onto the terrace. A cushioned two-seater was empty at the end of the long, paved area, next to potted trees that afforded privacy, and it was there that he halted, his mission accomplished.

"Sit down and I'll get us something to drink." She sat, surprised to find herself in the relatively quiet atmosphere, sheltered from the doors by plants that were spaced to create a degree of privacy. She looked up, surprised to see the stars, and realized that they were above the lights of the city, where the stars could be seen. Below, a faint hum of traffic could be heard; a horn blaring, muted in the distance. The music was muffled and then, as he came toward her again, he gently closed the terrace doors behind him and she no longer heard the voices that filled the apartment, the music reduced to a steady beat that vibrated in the floor beneath her feet.

"Thank you." He held out the tall glass and she took it, sipping at the drink that almost overflowed.

"Sorry, didn't get it on your dress, did I? I filled it up so I wouldn't have to go back right away."

"That's all right. It didn't spill." She looked at him and then quickly back at the drink that tasted faintly like lemonade, but with a tartness that told her lemon was only one ingredient.

His eyes were resting on her face and she felt the slow blush that began below the neckline of her dress. Thankful for the darkness on the terrace that would hide her from him, she ducked her head. "Would you like some of this food we confiscated?"

Wishing she would look at him again, he nodded. He still hadn't seen enough. A smile that dimpled, those incredible green eyes. She was like a breath of fresh air, her perfume a bouquet of spring flowers that blended with the clean scent of her hair as she lowered her head. He leaned closer and inhaled. Clean. That was it. She smelled clean, like the breeze that blew in his bedroom window, early in the morning when the sun rose over the east coast of Florida.

"Hmmm . . . good food . . ." He picked up the plate from the small patio table in front of them and handed it to her. "Here, you hold it . . . I'll feed us."

His fingers snatched up another of the chilly, pink shrimp and he dipped it into the spicy sauce before lifting it to his mouth. She watched as he ate it, amused at his obvious enjoyment and then laughed softly as he boyishly licked the tip of his index finger to catch the drop of cocktail sauce he had missed.

"Did we get napkins?" His hand traveled to his lap and she froze in place as he touched her leg, his fingers searching for the elusive napkin that had been covering the bottom of his glass.

She was warm, firm, her thigh tense at the touch of his palm against it, and without haste he lifted his hand. "I found it." Wet from the dampness on his glass, the napkin stuck to his fingers and he grinned as he wiped at his mouth.

"Let me go in and pick up a couple more. This could get messy."

She shook her head. "Thanks, no, I have one here," she said as she fished about, her fingers settling finally on the elusive napkin where it lay on the settee beside her. This is foolish, she thought. He touched my leg and I'm all fidgety. I should have eaten lunch . . . the drink he gave me is making me goofy. And I can't seem to swallow any of this food. The appetite that had been raging fifteen minutes ago had all but disappeared. The presence of the man next to her managed to drive away everything except her awareness of him; her nerves attuned to his every movement, her senses tingling as she felt the brush of his leg against hers, his fingers touching her as he reached in the shadows for the food on her plate.

"I'm afraid I didn't catch your name in there." He spoke through the cracker and dip he was biting into and she swallowed, finally getting rid of the bite-size sandwich she had been struggling with.

"We weren't introduced. They don't seem to do much of that. I haven't even seen Marcie since I got here. It looks like people just wander around on their own until they get paired up."

"Marcie?" Jeff's Marcie? This was the friend he had dragged his feet at meeting. Fool! "Are you here with anyone?"

Surprised, she looked up. "Oh, no! I'm just visiting Marcie for the week. I'm not really looking for anyone to . . . well, I mean I'm not really . . ."

"Neither am I." He grinned at her. "Jeff brought me along tonight, said he wanted me to meet Marcie's friend. I think that was you."

"Oh . . ." The word dragged out as she remembered Marcie's mumbled remark about a man. "I suspect he meant me. I'm Sara. From Goose Creek, South Carolina."

His grin widened and he wiped his hand upon the small napkin, scrubbing at a spot of sauce that lingered. "I'm pleased to meet you, Sara, from Goose Creek." Clean now, his hand sought hers and took the plate from her, leaning to place it on the table. He turned back and surveyed her. "What do you do in Goose Creek?"

She wished she could see him better. He was in shadow with the moon just over his left shoulder. Stars were dandy but they didn't provide much light. His blond hair was short and a little curly. She knew his eyes were dark, but she wanted to see the expression on his face. "Well, most of the time I work at a lawyer's office, typing, answering his phones, and keeping his files up to date. The rest of the time I keep house for my dad and brothers."

"Your mother?" His question was soft as he leaned closer, the mystery of her scent drawing him.

"She died years ago." The statement was a bare fact, and he sensed the pain behind it. He would leave it for now.

"I'm Cal. From Florida, not far from Silver Springs." He ventured a finger toward her, catching it in the wisp of hair that hung in a fragile curl in front of her ear. Her head swung toward him and his finger brushed her cheek, and then his hand cupped her chin as he tipped her head back. Between the moonglow and a slant of light from the terrace doors, she was illuminated before him. Eyes, enormous as they widened; lips, parted and soft, tremulous as they waited; and breath that whispered toward him as he lowered his mouth to hers.

He saw a trace of panic in her face and she stiffened as he moved toward her and then they touched and she shivered. His mouth was gentle, the warmth overcoming and banishing the chill she felt. With a sigh that whispered consent, she leaned closer and his lips asked more, shifting and seeking as he tasted the tart, lemony flavor of her drink. His head lifted and her eyes opened, blinking as she focused on him. The fear was gone, confusion in its place, and she fought the softening of her body even as she leaned toward him. He felt her instinctive retreat, knew that she was hesitant, but his appetite had been enhanced by her flavor and texture. And so, his mouth lowered to hers again as he sought once more the taste and scent of her.

Heat, fierce and unexpected, took her by surprise, spreading through her body and then accelerating to a beat that flooded her veins in a rapid staccato, taking her breath. He lifted his head and soothed her with a palm that flexed against her back, supporting her. His other hand was at the back of her head, his fingers winding through the mass of hair that was pinned securely in place. She felt him working gently at the pins, making short work of her twisted chignon, and then with a sigh, he pulled her closer and she felt the hair released, spreading over her shoulders and down her back.

"Cal?" The whisper was bewildered, hesitant.

"Shhh, it's all right." His own voice was steady, reassuring, but still she felt the rapid beat of his heart against her.

"Please, Cal. I don't belong here. I think I need to leave." She straightened and he released her, his hold gentle on her hands.

He watched a moment as she lifted her fingers from his and combed them through the curls that hung over her shoulders, and then he stopped her with a touch.

"Leave your hair down, it's all right like that." All right! It was magnificent! He cleared his throat and rose, drawing her with him, his fingers tightening as he watched her brush at her dress, smoothing the skirt with one hand as she edged toward the terrace doors.

"Come on, Sara. I'll take you home." His voice was gentle but determined, and he left her no choice as he guided her through the crowd and out the front door of the apartment.

TWO

Seldom in her life had Sara O'Brien been so impetuous. Silently, she raked herself over the coals, every moment aware of the man sitting next to her in the taxi. Dumb! Dumb! How could I be so foolish, she wondered, her eyes focused on the small patch of the city she could see from the front windshield of the cab. Somehow, it seemed wiser to look straight ahead, eyes determinedly averted from her companion, whose long, lean length was a bit too close for comfort. She caught glimpses of buildings, billboards that lined the street, some high above the roadway, lighted store windows, flashing neon signs that caught her eye, all casting a vari-colored glow on the man who sat next to her as the driver sped down the wide avenue.

"Sara?" He had waited, watching her withdraw from him as soon as the cab left the curb in front of the highrise apartment house. She was frightened, and for a moment Cal was amused. It had been a long time since he had deliberately attempted to arouse feelings of any kind in a woman. Now that he had a chance to enjoy his last couple of days in New York with a pretty girl, he had managed to scare her. "Sara, please look at me."

The soft, coaxing tones drew her. One hand, broad across the palm, with callouses that were hard against her fingers, twined gently with hers, and with the other he reached across her to grasp her shoulder. She turned at his silent urging and his smile was reassuring.

"I'm not in my element here, you know." It wasn't what he expected her to say and his eyebrow raised in question. "I mean, this is the first time I've been in New York City and I don't really fit in." He felt the faint tremble in her fingers and clasped them more securely. "Cal, I've never been to that kind of a party. I was out of place there. I've never kissed a man before that I didn't even know."

"Ah . . . but you didn't." He interrupted smoothly and she watched the smile broaden until his eyes were narrowed and creases deepened in his cheeks. "I kissed you, my dear girl. And that makes all the difference in the world. You needn't feel that you've compromised your virtue." His hand lifted hers slowly and surely to his lips and she felt the warmth of his breath against her skin. His mouth touched, like a whisper of butterfly wings against her hand, and then he released her, settling back in the corner of the seat.

"My virtue isn't in question." The words were spoken in accents that gave away her heritage. "I just wanted you to understand that I'm not a party girl. I didn't go there tonight to be picked up." She frowned. "I don't mean to sound ungrateful, though. I do appreciate you taking me home. I just . . ."

"Shhh . . . I won't tell if you don't," he teased. "The folks down in Goose Creek will never know that you left a rowdy affair with a stranger and allowed him liberties." His eyes were twinkling in the glitter of headlights that flashed in the window behind their heads and Sara laughed, her voice just a little husky, just a little nervous.

"Do you know where we are? How far from Marcie's apartment we are, I mean?"

"Vaguely. I've done some traveling in the city, but I wasn't driving. I'm afraid we're at the cab driver's mercy, Sara." He reached to touch a wisp of hair that fell against her cheek and tucked it back, his finger tracing the line of her jaw and then brushing against the waves that still cascaded over her shoulders. "I don't know why you don't wear your hair like this all the time, Sara. It's lovely, you know." His fingers were tangled in its length and he drew her closer.

"Little southern belle, let me taste you one more time before this evening ends." His mouth lowered to hers and touched the fullness of her lips, carefully, gently, holding back the surge of desire that beat through his body. She tasted like nothing he had ever known. She was fresh, sweet, unconsciously alluring and he drew back, wanting so much more, knowing with regret that she hovered on the edge of retreat.

Her eyes were open, wary and wide, and he saw again the hesitation in them. With a smile that reassured her, he leaned to whisper in her ear. "You're a genuine innocent, aren't you?"

She flushed and turned her head away. "Small town maybe, but I'm not a child, Cal."

The driver slowed and turned down a side street. They had left the bright lights and the buildings here were all apartments, one after another, lined up, Sara thought, like so many boxes in a row. For a moment, she yearned for home: the white house that sat in the center of a half acre surrounded by trees and porches, its homey rooms filled with comfortable furniture;

where her brothers argued amiably over the television, where her parents had raised four children, where she was surrounded by love.

The cab stopped and Cal opened the door and stepped out, reaching through the passenger window to hand the driver a folded bill. "Thanks. Don't wait for me." He tugged at Sara's hand and smiled at her hesitation. Her eyes traveled from Cal to the cab driver. Once the taxi left, she was on her own and the man who watched her with an amused grin was well aware of her problem. It would be downright rude to leave him standing at the curb. Besides, she wasn't sure she wanted to find her way through the corridors of the building to Marcie's apartment, unescorted. It was very late, very dark, and the building looked very deserted. A few lights filtered through draped windows, the recessed bulbs cast a dim light in the foyer and the small lobby was empty.

While she stood at the curb, pondering her choices, the taxi pulled away, scattering bits of paper and debris in its wake. She shrugged. Cal was by far the lesser risk. With a grin that took him by surprise, she turned toward the building, her fingers searching in the small bag she carried, looking for the key Marcie had provided her with.

"I hope you can find a cab when you come back down. They seem to be few and far between in this neighborhood." She was pleased with her nonchalant tone of voice. It was much smoother than the erratic beat of her heart, much calmer than the trembling fingers that were giving her a problem as she attempted to fit the key into the door.

"Here, let me do that." He eased the key from her, noting the quickly drawn breath, the subtle shrinking of her body as he crowded her in the small entryway.

With a careful touch on her arm, he drew her through the open door and turned her toward the elevator.

"Sixth floor, right?" At her raised eyebrow, he lifted the key and waved it beneath her nose. 612. The number was there in small, raised detail. Marcie's apartment number.

"I didn't realize it was on the key." She reached for it, but it was too late. He slipped it into his pocket and then as the elevator door slid open, he reached to hold it while she stepped inside. His hand lifted, one long finger touched the button and the elevator shuddered into motion. Sara backed into the wall for balance as Cal reached automatically for her arm.

"Okay?" He faced her and she nodded quickly as she eyed his brown shirt, focusing on the button that was level with her nose.

He chuckled softly. "Don't look so frightened, child. I'm only a Florida cowboy, not a big-city slicker." His eyes caught the apprehension she tried to conceal, the rapid pulse that beat visibly in the hollow of her throat, and the flush that crept up to settle on the fine bones that shaped her cheeks. With gentle words, he teased her and was rewarded with a smile that trembled on her lips.

"I'm not frightened, Cal. Not really. I don't think I could explain how I feel. I'm not sure I . . ." The elevator stopped and she turned to the right as the doors slid shut behind them. Marcie's apartment was a few feet down the hall and without comment, he unlocked the door and eased her inside. Without hesitation, he followed her and leaned against the door, closing it securely. His hand held the key, dangling it between two fingers and she took it from him.

"Thank you. I appreciate you bringing me up here. These hallways are probably very safe, but I'm a little uneasy at night.'' She watched him, her eyes unsure, the pupils dilated in the dim light of the vestibule. A small lamp, around the corner in the living room, glowed softly and she stood silhouetted in its light. She was substance and shadow, her slender body curved and tempting in the half-light and Cal felt a tug of desire that brought him a step closer to her.

One large hand lifted to touch her face, traced the line of her cheek and dropped to her throat. His work-roughened fingers touched the spot where her pulse still beat raggedly and then he slid the length of his hand through her hair to the nape of her neck, where he curved it to fit beneath the curls. She was small, vulnerable, and tempting, and with all of the control within his grasp, he leaned toward her.

His mouth touched hers softly, his lips teased at hers until they parted and he tasted the sweetness of her breath. Then, with tender, careful touches, he kissed her; moving to her cheek, up to whisper across her temple, and then with a deep breath that made him aware of her scent, her distinctive, elusive perfume, her hair that curled against his mouth and received his kiss without her knowing, he inhaled her essence and for a moment closed his eyes. For just a moment, he was tempted. And then his large hands closed on her shoulders and he stepped back.

''Thank you, Sara. I've enjoyed being with you tonight.''

A look that might have been relief, mixed with disappointment flitted across her face and then she smiled. ''I appreciate your bringing me back here, Cal.'' She laughed, the sound light and pleasing, and her smile was relieved. ''I've already said that, haven't I?''

''It's okay, Sara. Call it my good deed for the day.'' He reached behind him for the doorknob and with a

small salute he was gone, and she quickly slid the dead-
bolt home and slid the chain in place. She leaned on
the door and closed her eyes. He could have stayed and
she would have let him. She would have made coffee,
perhaps, and sat with him, talking and . . . With a
start, she moved from the door, shaking her head. Ships
that pass in the night. She would never see him again.
A pang of regret touched her. He could have been
important; he had reached her, touched her, made her
aware. For the first time in too long, she had been
aware of her own quiet appeal. She had seen and
appreciated the approval in his eyes, had felt the tugs
of desire and rising passion that were almost unknown
to her.

Her head dropped and her shoulders slumped wearily. The week in New York was over and she faced
the return trip home tomorrow. Cal had rescued the
evening for her, had turned an uncomfortable situation
into an interlude that would remain in her memory long
after she returned home. She touched her lips with fingertips that had lingered against his chest, then had
traveled to his shoulders, aware of the strength he kept
under control, aware of the muscles that flexed beneath
the brown shirt that hid pure masculinity.

Having three older brothers was an education in
itself. Not much about the male body was a mystery to
Sara. She had seen the well-formed bodies of men
daily, had lived with specimens of manhood who had
set numerous female hearts fluttering. As hers had fluttered tonight. A smile, wistful and brief, touched her
lips and was gone. She straightened and moved into the
living room, conscious of the heavy length of her hair
as the dark waves and curls spread over her shoulders
and down her back.

"I don't know why you don't wear your hair like

this all the time. It's lovely, you know.'' His words came back as if recorded in her memory bank. She shook her head in dismissal of his suggestion. Sara O'Brien kept all of her femininity closely guarded. It was easier that way.

"What do you mean, she's gone?" The man definitely was irritated, thought Marcie with a grin.

"Just what I said. She left for the airport over an hour ago." She repeated the words for the second time and waited for his retort. It came immediately.

"Why didn't she tell me she was leaving? I just saw her last night. I brought her home and she never mentioned that she would be leaving today." His words were clipped and angry. "Look," his voice changed, became softer and coaxing. "Can you give me her address? Her last name?"

"O'Brien . . ." Marcie chewed the inside of her mouth meditatively as she twirled the coil of her telephone cord around her index finger. "Look, let me do this," she began. "I'll write her and give her your name and address and if she wants to hear from you, she can go on from there. I'll tell her you called . . ."

"Hell's bells! What is the big deal? I'm not about to kidnap the girl, I just want to see her again!" He was adamant, pacing the apartment to the limit of the phone cord, one hand holding the receiver to his ear, the other holding the base of the unit, waving it in the air to emphasize his words. His frustration was genuine.

Early in the morning, before the sun rose, he had stretched and yawned, aware that sleep was elusive to the point of being almost nonexistent. The hours tossing and turning on Jeff's studio couch had been nonproductive. He had argued with himself at first. She was young, innocent, definitely not his style. She would not fit into the category of female he was interested in. She spelled trouble and he congratulated himself on his escape.

Then, as the hours dragged on, he began to tally up his record. For years, since Vietnam, relationships had been sporadic at best. Women were always available if he felt the urge, but somehow he had been able to submerge himself into the ranch and the brief alliances that had been part of his life had dwindled until they almost seemed to be more trouble than they were worth. A woman so easily acquired had little value and he had begun to feel himself cheapened by his use of them. The female population of the small town near his ranch was sparse, especially the available singles. Married women were off-limits, always had been. He had been selective in his dating, knowing that he wasn't ready to offer a future that included marriage.

Marriage . . . he had considered it once. His mouth became a grim line and his eyes narrowed as he remembered his youthful fling with hearts and flowers.

LouAnn, even the name conjured up bitter memories of deception and anguish. He'd been so sure of her: of her innocence, of her wholehearted desire for the life they would share. Until her brother had let it slip during a poker game that LouAnn was seeing the local banker's son. While Cal played poker, LouAnn was playing footsies with young Mr. Moneybags.

It didn't bother him anymore, he realized. Her choice was logical. Cal would never be rich, maybe comfortable and secure . . . someday. For LouAnn, someday was too far off in the future. While Cal toiled on the ranch, she enticed the very eligible Caleb Martin and when faced with her duplicity, she had shrugged and laughed at his pain.

Her innocent blue eyes were knowing as she patted

his cheek. "Maybe we can get together sometime, Cal. I've always wondered how you'd be . . ." And for the first and only time in his life, Cal had wanted to raise his hand to a woman.

Fists clenched against the urge, he had ground his teeth and his voice was a growl. "Whores aren't my style, lady."

LouAnn flinched. His words had stung but she recovered quickly and tilted her head at an arrogant angle. "Too bad, cowboy," she purred. "You just turned down the best chance you ever had."

He had watched her walk out of his life. And every step that she took renewed his determination that marriage would only be an option if he found a woman he could trust. A woman who would . . .

He shook his head in disgust. He hadn't thought about LouAnn in years. He didn't have time. Work filled the daylight hours. He whiled away the darkness by eating and sleeping and an occasional game of poker in the bunkhouse with his men, usually dropping wearily into his bed by ten o'clock, aware that his internal alarm would waken him before five in the morning. Maybe in a few more years he would find a woman that fit into his existence. A farm girl, perhaps; willing to keep his house comfortable, his bed warm, and give him children before he was too old to enjoy being a father.

A vision of dark curls that had clung to his fingers, green eyes that glowed with a gentle warmth, and a rounded figure that had for a moment melted against him swept across his mind. Sara. Definitely not Florida ranch material. Little southern belle.

His lips lifted in a smile as he remembered her fragile innocence. No, she had no place in his life. She would require wooing, her kind expected courting. He shook his head and closed his eyes again. The faint sounds of the city vibrated outside the well-insulated apartment, but they penetrated his determined effort to sleep. And finally, as the sky began to change from murky grey to the faintest shades of pink in the east, across the river that ran to the ocean, beyond the skyscrapers that towered in the half-light, he stood on his feet and admitted defeat.

All arguments to the contrary, she was worth at least a day of his time. Then he could forget her and go home, savor one day with her and then go back to Florida. Six cups of coffee later, newspapers scattered across the kitchen table, Jeff in the shower, and the *Today* show on the television, he approached the telephone.

Almost nine o'clock, they would be up. Sara looked like an early riser and Marcie probably would be up, keeping her company. But the words that assailed him without mercy put a stop to his plans.

She was gone, had caught an early flight, and he was sure he caught a trace of smug satisfaction in Marcie's voice as she gave him the news. With barely civil tones, he slowly told her his address, spelled his last name, and told her goodbye.

"Problems?" Jeff was tall and husky in briefs that rode low on his hips, a towel slung around his neck as he ran his hands through dark, curly hair that was almost dry. The growl that served as a reply was unexpected. Cal was upset, worse yet, he looked as if his anger was directed at Jeff.

"Whoa, old boy!" The words were delivered in a patient voice that belied Jeff's anxious expression.

"She'll give her my address!" He stalked to the window and his glare ignored the sunshine that warmed him. Fingers deep in his pockets, he rocked back on his heels. "If, and that's a big if, if she wants to hear from me, she can get in touch." He turned to Jeff, his face a study in aggravation, brows lowered over eyes that glared with frustration.

"Is this display a direct result of your disappearance from the party last night?" A grin that could only be described as pleased turned up the corners of Jeff's mobile lips; his eyes danced with glee and his words were a teasing drawl. "Thought you weren't interested in meeting Marcie's friend? Parties are boring. Watching the Mets on television is your idea of entertainment, remember?"

Hands that were calloused where reins rubbed against them, hands that were more accustomed to touching animals than humans, raised in a gesture of defeat and Cal shook his head. "So, for once I was off base." The anger, easily born of his frustration, just as easily died as he answered Jeff's grin. "Miss Magnolia Blossom deserves a second look." His words were offhand, but the eyes of his friend saw beneath the flip retort.

"Got to you, didn't she?" The exodus from the party had been noted by both Jeff and Marcie and only fast talking on his part had kept Marcie from chasing after the departing pair.

"She's just a baby, Jeff. He'll scare her to death." He had laughed derisively, but the unmistakable sincerity in her eyes had halted his reaction.

"Not old Cal. He's a southern gentleman. Beneath that rough cowboy exterior beats a heart of true gentility. Don't worry about your friend, Marcie. If she left here a lady, Cal will deliver her to your door intact." His words were meant to comfort her and Marcie accepted them gladly. The party was just getting underway nicely and as much as she loved Sara, babysitting was not on the schedule for tonight. Maybe being alone with a good-looking man would do her good. She sure needed to get out of her shell. With that thought, Marcie had turned to her newest conquest and with a brilliant smile, laid her glossy fingertips on his shoulder as she invited him to dance.

"Cal . . ." Jeff's voice trailed off as he pondered on the form his query should take. "Did you deliver Magnolia in one piece?"

"Is this kiss-and-tell time, Jeff?" The grin was derisive now. "I'll expect the same report on your evening, you know."

"Hey, just checking!" The dark, curly head ducked and Jeff headed for the bedroom. Marcie might be important and he decided their evening was too private to share, even with his best friend.

Without looking, he sensed the presence of Cal behind him as he jerked on his jeans. "Do you think she'll get in touch with you?" He glanced over his shoulder and caught a strangely vulnerable look that flitted across the tanned features.

Shoulders lifted in a gesture that almost eliminated the need of a reply. "Who knows. Maybe it isn't such a good idea, anyway. I've got enough to occupy my time at the ranch without getting involved with a kid. Especially one who lives five hundred miles from where I do business."

"Want me to find out more about her?" The offer was tentative and Cal eyed him for a moment, hesitant as he pondered it.

"No. Let it go." He straightened and stood just inside the bedroom doorway, the decision made. Forget the southern belle, enjoy the last day in New York, and then go back to Florida and the ranch that was, of necessity, the number-one priority in his life.

*   *   *

The flight was bumpy, the food was terrible, plastic and lukewarm, but Sara hardly noticed. She leaned back in the seat and closed her eyes.

A face, hard and weathered, with eyes that had pierced her protective shield almost effortlessly, swam before her. Lines that appeared when he smiled relieved the harshness of his countenance. Lips that had touched hers softly, coaxing her response, tasting her with whispering kisses that had brought pleasure of a sort she had not associated with kissing. She sighed and the smile that accompanied her involuntary, yearning sound brought an interested look to the face of the businessman who occupied the seat next to her.

She was immune to his glances, her mind taken up with the man who had precipitated her early departure from New York. Marcie had been surprised at her early-morning evacuation.

"I think I'd better go home a day early, Marcie. I need to get things done before I go back to work." Even to her own ears the excuse sounded weak, but Marcie accepted it without question. There was no use in arguing with Sara when she made up her mind and this morning was no exception. The reservation had been changed before the sun rose and she was firm in her decision to leave. With a hug and promises to keep in touch, the women parted at the apartment door and with a wave, Sara had entered the elevator.

Now, the plane began its descent and the familiar network of roads appeared beneath her window as she watched for the triangle formed by St. James Boulevard and Highway 52, which contained the stores and offices that made up Goose Creek. The cars crept along on narrow streets and the sleepy town spread beneath her. Most of its working inhabitants either went to the nearby military bases to work or else headed downtown to the city of Charleston, which lay on a peninsula of land formed by the Ashley and Cooper Rivers.

She felt the familiar sense of quiet joy as she envisioned going home. Churches, schools, grocery stores, the library, specialty shops, and the K–Mart sprawled beneath her in the sunshine, all were part of the safe, secure life she had known for years. The lawyer's office she worked in was just west of the center of town, in a fairly new complex that housed a dentist and doctor in the same building.

Safe, secure; she decided those were good words to describe her life. Nothing wrong with that, she thought as she began to gather her belongings. Cal didn't belong here. He was about as far from safety as she had gotten in years. Four years to be exact, since graduation night in Goose Creek. Marcie had hit the nail on the head when she mentioned that night.

It was an evening she had tried, without success, to forget. An evening that had changed her life forever. A bitter sadness filled her as she prepared to leave the plane and her mind was flooded with the memory of the night the president of her high-school senior class had, without tenderness, without a trace of regret, taken her innocence and left her with a nightmare that four years later still haunted her dreams.

THREE

The horse was skittish, ears flicking back and forth, his rear end dancing from side to side. The reins tightened a bit. A husky, whispering sound caught his attention and the quarter horse tossed his head again, eager to be moving at a faster pace. Again, wordless sounds issued from the man's throat and the powerful body surged as the horse obeyed his master's signal. His muscles bunched and gathered as his legs stretched out and ate up the distance that lay between the long, low barn and the stand of trees across the pasture.

A stream, shallow but almost twenty-feet wide, wended its way beneath the overhanging limbs of the oaks and willows that lined its banks. The oasis was populated by black and white cattle, many of them almost knee-deep in the cool water, moving placidly among the rocks, making their way to the far side of the pasture. The sun was well above the eastern horizon. It had risen before six and with a quick glance at his watch, Cal noted that it was already past eight o'clock. The morning was half over and he had had a late start. He rode at a slower pace, his horse trotting among the cows, ignored by them as they headed for the heavier grass that lay beyond the stream.

"This sure beats New York." The observation was spoken with a satisfied growl and the horse cast a quick look back at the rider. A gloved hand reached absently to tug at the coarse brown mane and the equally dark head bent as if to acknowledge the rough caress. Acres of grassy, rolling pasture land spread before him and Cal breathed deeply of the clean air as he narrowed his eyes to follow the straight line of fence that stretched out before him. He laid the reins against his horse's neck, and obediently the animal turned to follow the string of barbed wire that was attached at intervals to posts that had taken weeks to install.

A half-smile curved the corner of his lips as he rode the fence line, leaving the herd behind him. This, the eastern boundary of his land, was too close to the barns and the house he lived in, but it couldn't be helped. Years before, in hard times that had almost caused his defeat, Cal's father had sold off almost half of his property. The money realized by the sale had pulled the ranch back from the edge of disaster, paid off the loans at the bank, and purchased new stock. But the reminder of his father's brush with bankruptcy thinned his lips and the smile that had flirted across his mouth vanished. He pulled up short and watched as a lone rider moved into his range of vision. The tall figure sat straight in his saddle and the reins lay loosely in his hands, his horse taking directions from the pressure of the rider's knees.

"Hyatt." The word was a greeting, accompanied by a short nod as the two horses neared, their courses intersecting at the boundary fence. His neighbor was a few years older than himself, but Cal knew that the relaxed stance and hat pushed back casually concealed a body that was lean and hard, a mind that was sharp and keen. The tanned features bore the look of years of hard work; the nose sharp, a little crooked, eyes deepset and piercing in their scrutiny, and a mouth that seldom smiled.

"Morning, Les." His own greeting was equally terse. There was no grudge between the men, simply the knowledge that Cal resented another man on property that circumstances had decreed would not be part of his inheritance. Les Cochrane was a decent man, a widower with two children, a hard worker. His only fault was his proximity, a reminder to Cal that ranching was an occupation fraught with obstacles.

Too much rain, not enough rain, disease, high vet bills, the rising cost of feed; all had contributed to his father's problems. The final blow had come while Cal was in Nam: a rare winter icestorm that had caught the ranchers unaware. Calves, dropped by cows unused to the cold weather too far from the barn to reach safety, had died before the hands had been able to find them and bring them to shelter. It had been a disaster, the finishing touch that had bowed the elderly rancher's head in defeat.

Cal's arrival home from Vietnam a year later had brought new life to Jim Hyatt. But years of hard work, sorrow over the death of his wife, and the knowledge that he had sold half of his son's inheritance in order to keep his head above water had taken his strength and the pneumonia that struck him in the middle of January was too powerful for his weary body to overcome. Cal had buried his father in the small cemetery in town, in a grave next to the mother he barely remembered. Then, he had straightened his shoulders, dug in his heels, and worked as if the demons of hell were at his back. Day after day, week after week and finally he began to count time by years as he fought to build the ranch that had all but slipped away from his family.

Now, hardened by the years, his body strong and healthy, he rode the fences and eyed with barely-concealed avarice, the property he hoped to include one day in his holdings.

"Heard you went to New York." The words were an understatement.

The small community had buzzed with speculation when Cal Hyatt took a vacation. His usual two-day trips to buy cattle a couple of times a year were commonplace. Fellow ranchers followed somewhat the same schedule and he often traveled with one of them or met friends at stock sales. A trip north, spending a week in New York City just for a vacation was a rarity and the neighborhood had been alive with speculation. His return had been quiet and within twenty-four hours he had resumed his usual schedule, ending the rumors that had him marrying a beautiful model or selling his ranch to a huge conglomerate. He smiled now.

"Thought I deserved a few days off." His hand reached automatically for the pocket that held his cigarettes and he lit one, peering through the smoke to catch Les's reaction.

"Don't we all." His horse danced sideways and Les pulled back on the reins, holding his mount steady. "Checking out fences this morning?" His hands were large, brown and lean, and he shifted one to rest against his thigh, leaning to nod at the fence line that ran into the distance as far as they could see. A knoll, more than half-a-mile distant hid the running wire from their sight and Cal nodded as he narrowed his eyes, checking the tautness of the wires as they ran from one post to the next.

His nod was brief. "My hands are busy with other

things.'' He turned his horse easily with a twitch of the reins and nodded a farewell as he touched the rim of his hat with his index finger. "Give my regards to your boys. Tell them to stop by.''

With an identical salute, Les turned away and touched his heels to the sides of his black gelding. Without hesitation the horse broke into a lope that carried him smoothly away in the direction of his own barns and ranch house.

Cal gave his bay tacit permission to move out and the horse took advantage of his slack hold to celebrate his exuberance. Within seconds the magnificent animal was stretched low, hooves reaching eagerly as he ate up the distance to the hill just ahead of them. Instinctively, Cal's fingers tightened on the reins and then with a grin, he bent low and let his enthusiasm for the morning match that of his horse. For just a few minutes, he thought. His body had harnessed its desires too long and this sense of freedom, a gift of the sunshine and blue skies, begged to be expressed.

And so, the horse and man became one creature in that moment and melded as they raced to the low summit before them. At its peak, Cal reined in and spoke in a soft voice to his mount. His eyes flicked over the familiar landscape before him, the fence line stretching out in an unending thread, the pasture behind him, still green with early summer rains, the ranch house in the distance. His. Satisfaction gleamed in his smile and he sat back easily in his saddle.

I'd like to bring her here, show her this. The thought sprang full-blown into his mind and he blinked at its intrusion. Sara . . . she'd been hiding there, in the far corners, making herself known at odd moments, then without warning her face would swim in his memory, her scent would tease his nostrils and with his eyes closed, he could almost see her. Little green eyes, he thought, you've stuck to me like a sand burr. No not quite, more like an elusive thread that clings and won't be brushed off. For as often as he tried to flush her from his thoughts, she returned, when he was least ready, when he was vulnerable, tired, sleepy, relaxed. When his body and mind were most content, she crept in and he felt the warmth of her, the softness of her mouth under his, the curling cloud of dark hair that had clung to his fingers.

He shook his head and touched the horse with his heels. Sara O'Brien was an incident that needed to be put into its proper perspective. An evening out of time, a pleasant memory . . . Forget it, Hyatt. Get to work and forget her. If she wanted to see you again, she could have written or called or something. She's not your type, she's not tough enough for your life.

A frown settled into place and the lines in his forehead stole the look of pleasure he had worn a few minutes earlier. The horse moved into a trot that carried him down the knoll and he began the time-consuming task of riding his fences.

It was late in the afternoon when he returned to the barn and the sun was hot against his shirt, warming his skin through the denim and chambray he wore. He swung from the saddle and with quick movements stripped the horse of its tack, shaking out the blanket and lifting the heavy saddle easily as he carried it inside. The bay followed, reins slack as they looped over Cal's arm and then with a brush and a rough cloth the horse and man renewed their acquaintance. Long strokes and muttered confidences blended as the animal was groomed and the man bent to his task. Finally, he switched the bridle for a halter and with a slap against the shiny rump, he sent the horse into the corral.

Then he watched for a minute as the animal shook himself and then moved to stand beneath a tree where a watering trough spilled invitingly. The constant trickle of water that splattered in from a pipe extended at one end guaranteed fresh water for his animals. Cal was gratified as he watched the horse drink in great gulps, water sparkling as he threw his head back and shook the excess from his nose.

The walk to his ranch house was short, the path smooth and he unbuttoned his shirt as he went, anticipating the bucket of water that waited for him on the back porch. Bess knew he was coming, she had seen him ride in and the clean, cool water was ready. Aware of the fact that it was foolish, that a bathroom stood just inside the back door, with facilities more than able to meet his needs, he looked forward to his daily splash. As he stood at the side of the porch, his large hands cupped the water, raising it to his face. He blinked and shook his head, unknowingly mocking the actions of his horse in the corral. Another double handful sloshed against his forehead and his hands raked it through the sandy curls that darkened with dampness. Another cool drenching of his face followed and his head hung dripping over the pail as his bare forearms were rinsed. Then, with his head tilted back, he shook the excess off and reached for the hand towel that Bess had left for him. With a grin he emptied the bucket, spraying the water across the small patch of petunias Bess had planted by the porch and lay the towel over the edge of the railing to dry.

There were four steps and he took them in two, across the wide porch and then the screen door slammed behind him as he strode into the kitchen. Checkered curtains matched the oilcloth that covered the long, rustic table, benches on either side, a single, heavy wooden armchair at each end. He took in the kitchen at a glance, a pot bubbling on the burner, the coffee pot perking, and a place set at the end of the table closest to the stove. Bread, thickly sliced and crusty, sat on a wooden board next to a bowl of applesauce. He grunted in satisfaction and slid into the chair.

"Bess! Get your beautiful body in here and feed me!" The words roared from him as he leaned back in the maple armchair, his fists lined up at the edge of the table. The woman who filled the doorway behind him moved at her own pace. No way would Callen Hyatt disrupt her schedule. The fact that her life revolved around him, keeping him well fed, cleanly clothed, and comfortable was beside the point. Her appraisal was swift. He looked to be in a good mood, a rather rare occurrence lately.

"Don't get smart, boy. Not unless you want to wear this stew." Her words were dry and flat, her voice husky. Her movements were economical as she reached in front of him for the large bowl that sat on his plate and filled it at the stove with the savory mixture that featured beef and vegetables. It steamed invitingly as she replaced the bowl before him and his fingers captured her wrist before she could withdraw.

His mood had changed and his eyes flickered over her as he leaned back to face her. "Hey! Everything all right?"

The woman brushed his shirt with broad fingers and dropped her hand, her other wrist still held by him—the grip gentle. "If I didn't have to hold your lunch till supper time, things would be better. You need to eat regular, Cal." Her voice scolded him, its husky force at odds with the body that had given out on her lately.

Bess Kettering had always been there for Cal, had

helped to raise him, had cleaned his ears and boxed them on occasion, had welcomed him home after Nam, had comforted him on the day of his father's funeral. Her solid bulk was as much a part of his life as the ranch that nurtured them both. She was as close to a mother as he would ever have, as good a friend as he could ever find, and she loved him with a fierce, protective passion that he had only been aware of in the last few years.

Widowed early in her twenties, she had lived here—childless, without a man in her life that Cal knew of—and through the years had made a home out of the house they lived in. She was constant; caring for him, for his mother and father before their deaths, and the transient men who had worked here.

True, he had a bunkhouse for the hands, but meals were eaten here, in the kitchen that was Bess's domain. Her booming voice could cut down a rambunctious youngster, her quick wit could engage the men in teasing exchanges, and her old-fashioned cooking could feed the hard-working cowhands that came and went with the seasons. But her mother's heart was given in unstinting devotion to Cal, the son she had never had. His welfare was her prime concern and she dug now at his reticence.

"Kinda glum these days, aren't you?"

"Changing the subject, Bess? I want to know how you're feeling. What did the doctor say yesterday?" He hid his concern with nonchalance as he bent to the stew, stirring it with his spoon and lifting a bite to his mouth.

"Is this twenty questions, Cal? I'll tell you if you tell me?" She retrieved her hand from him and rested her wide palms on her ample hips, a smile chasing across her face. "You haven't been yourself since you came back from New York, you know. Oh, you smile and talk to the men. You sit and watch the television screen at night, but sometimes you don't even notice when the program's over. You've got something on your mind. Or someone.''

The last two words hung in the silence between them and he flicked a quick glance at her as he reached for a piece of bread. ''Tell me about your visit at the doctor's office, Bess.'' The words were uncompromising and she knew the look on his face. He would get it from her, or he would call the doctor.

''I need a little surgery one of these days. Nothing important, nothing urgent. When things aren't so busy I'll take a few days off and get it taken care of.'' Her shrug dismissed the matter as if it were of little importance.

''What kind of surgery?''

He left no room for her to quibble and she grimaced in defeat. ''Just a bothersome gall bladder. Nothing to worry about if I watch what I eat.'' The fact that her healthy body had betrayed her frustrated Bess. She was strong, sturdy, and only fifty-five years old. Too young for the flat-out orders the doctor had given. Surgery, before it got to an emergency situation. But Cal needn't know that stipulation. Her smile lifted his mood and he leaned back, the buttered bread forgotten for a moment.

''I don't mean to be glum,'' he drawled, using her own word. ''I've had things on my mind.''

Her eyebrow raised in question. ''Just things? Not someone?'' Her laugh was teasing. ''I remember when you were smitten with the Bronson girl back a few years. You had the same look . . .''

''Forget it, Bess. Your imagination is working overtime.'' He dismissed her idea and turned back to his delayed lunch. It was good and he was hungry, and

Bess might be right. He needed to either do something about Sara or forget her, once and for all. Again, her green eyes mocked him and he pushed back his bowl, shoved his chair away from the table, and stood to his feet.

Bess was right. Sara was under his skin and he couldn't get her out of his mind. Time to take another look at the southern belle, maybe see if her taste was as addictive as he remembered, see if her curves were as soft and tempting as his body recalled.

His look dared Bess to question him as he left the room and took the stairs two at a time. She watched him go and shook her head over the stew, half-eaten. She heard the thump of the attic door overhead and she listened as faint footsteps echoed on the stairway to the third floor.

In seconds he was back down to the carpeted hallway and she heard him call down the stairway to the kitchen hallway. "Bess, where's my blue shirt?"

"Hanging in the sewing room. I had to replace a button." She looked puzzled for a moment and shrugged. Hard to tell what he was up to now. Whatever it was, she'd know soon enough.

Soon enough was just an hour later. Callen Hyatt once more left his ranch, overnight bag in the trunk, and a determined look on his face.

"Sara, smile for me," her brother wheedled softly as he leaned his chin on her shoulder. He had approached her quietly as she stood before the kitchen stove, poking disinterestedly at the bacon that fried in the skillet.

"Patrick! You startled me." She waved at him with the fork and he ducked.

"Just thought I'd get a rise out of you. You looked

so unhappy standing there.'' He leaned against the sink
and hooked his thumbs into the back of his jeans, eye-
ing her with concern. ''Was New York so tempting?
Are you yearning for the big city, little sister?'' His
voice was teasing, but it held an undercurrent of caring
that touched her.

''Just thinking, Patrick.'' Her grin was bright as she
took up the bacon and drained it on the paper towels
she had folded on a plate. ''Do you want two or three
eggs this morning?''

''Two.'' His gaze touched on her briefly, noting the
shadows under her eyes, the slender figure that had
lost a little of its roundness. ''Not talking, Sara?'' He
prompted her, determined to get an answer.

For four weeks he and his brothers had watched her.
Four weeks of Sara being not quite herself. A little
somber, her eyes lacking their usual sparkle, her
responses to their casual teasing not quite as quick and
biting. Something had happened to her in New York.
Jonathan was sure of it and he was seldom wrong in
his judgments. Dennis, the youngest O'Brien brother,
said that Sara needed a boyfriend. Perhaps, but Patrick
was skittish when it came to that area of his sister's
life.

Too well he remembered the high school romance
that had bloomed so briefly and faded as rapidly, leaving her pale and unhappy after graduation. All of their
questions had been turned away unanswered and they
had watched their beloved sister throughout that summer as she moved quietly through the house, smiling
gently, her eyes bleak. Finally, as if to put away her
youth and embark upon adulthood, she took a job at
the law office, bought a new wardrobe, and was once
more their Sara.

The Sara that fixed his breakfast this morning was

too reminiscent of that summer four years ago, and Patrick made a quick decision.

"Say!" It was his standard beginning when he wanted something and Sara grinned knowingly at him.

"Ask away, brother. I'm free for the day." She placed his plate in front of him and sat down across the table, holding her coffee mug with both hands. "Do you know that I spend half of my week wishing it were Saturday? And here I am offering my valuable time off to you."

He handed her a piece of bacon and picked up his fork. "You know me too well, sis." He ate half the scrambled eggs in three bites and then looked up at her. Her green eyes were soft, a half-smile played across her lips as she watched him. Patrick was her favorite brother, they shared a bond somehow that took nothing away from the love she felt for Jonathan and Dennis.

He spoke between bites. "I'm in a sort of bind. For tonight."

She drew back warily. "No blind dates, Patrick."

"This is almost an emergency, Sara. Tom asked me to go to a concert at the auditorium with him and I forgot that I had already asked Debbie to go into Charleston for dinner." He felt the old childhood urge to cross his fingers as he spoke. Telling a lie made him feel uncomfortable, even for a good cause. Granted, Tom had tickets for a concert, but had only called him late last night after a client had given him the tickets. Patrick's suggestion that Tom ask Sara had not been well received.

"Are you kidding, Pat? I've been after your sister for a date for three years and she won't give me a tumble. I've given up there." His words were tinged with anger. Sara had attracted him since she left her teens, when he decided she was old enough for him to date. At twenty-six he didn't want to be accused of robbing the cradle. The innocent demeanor of Patrick's sister appealed to him. She would be an ideal wife: pretty, a good cook, all the qualities he was seeking. The thought of waking up with her every morning for the rest of his life was enough to make Tom ready to give up his bachelorhood in a hurry.

"Let me see what I can do to help you use those tickets tomorrow night." His voice was soft against the receiver and Tom agreed easily.

"Good luck, pal. But I won't hold my breath waiting."

"Oh, Patrick!" Her moan was weary. "Don't start that again with Tom."

"Just one date, honey. I hate to leave him in the lurch like this. Do me a favor, will you, and listen to the music with him like a good girl." He met her eyes and felt only a tinge of guilt at his duplicity. "Sara, he's a nice guy. You need to get out and have some fun." He looked back down at his plate and wondered where all the eggs had gone. "Please, Sara. For me."

The request tore at her. Patrick never asked anything of her and she knew he was concerned about her. "Oh, all right." She stood up and reached for his plate. "Tell him to call me."

With a smile that he tried valiantly to hide from his sister, Patrick rose, his chair teetering on two legs before it settled back to the floor as he headed for the telephone in the hallway.

"Could you make me a couple more eggs, sis? Somebody ate mine."

It wasn't fair, Sara thought. Tom was a nice man. He had done all the right things: picked her up in his new car, brought her a bouquet of daisies that pleased her enormously, and had spent the evening being gentlemanly and eager to please. She should be enjoying the attention. He had been careful to only touch her when the need arose, taking her hand when she got out of the car, holding her elbow as they climbed the steps to the auditorium, his palm warm on her back as he guided her through the crowd in the lobby. But he had sensed her instinctive withdrawal and she had been mildly surprised herself as she realized what she was doing. It wasn't fair. She should be able to feel an attraction to him. But she didn't.

The night in New York had given her hope that the right man might appeal to her, that her aversion to the touch of any male, other than her family, might be a thing of the past.

Old brown shirt had done more than touch her. She flushed and turned her head to look out the car window. Much more. She ran the tip of her tongue over the outline of her lips as she remembered how his own had gained entry so easily. Her softness had fit snugly against his muscular body and for a short time she had been changed. From the reserved woman who had lived in her body for four years, Sara had been transformed into a young girl again; charmed by the stranger who had led her from the party to the balcony, from there to a taxi, and then to Marcie's apartment. All without a whimper of protest on her part. She shook her head in disbelief at the memory.

"What is it, Sara?" Tom's voice called her back from her reverie and she turned quickly to face him in the darkened car. He had pulled up in the driveway of her home and sat watching her quietly. The hands that had touched her lightly several times during the evening were fastened to the steering wheel. Then the right one left its position and he reached for her with it, grasping her fingers and lifting her left hand. He traced the length of her slender fingers idly and she watched him, wondering if she could get out of the car without a good-night kiss.

Dating in high school had been easy, first dates rated one kiss. But she was twenty-two years old, far beyond the rules that made life simple then, and she suspected that Tom had long-range plans where she was concerned. Her innate spirit of generosity and kindness dictated that she should be warm and appreciative of Tom's efforts for her enjoyment this evening. But the thought of his body against hers caused a chill to envelop her and the image of his hands touching her and his mouth against hers brought the metallic taste of fear into her throat. Not for the first time, she silently cursed the automatic reaction of her body and senses to the presence of a man.

"Don't look so afraid of me, Sara." He interrupted her thoughts again and she felt guilty.

"I'm not, Tom. Really." And she wasn't, not when she thought about it and realized that Tom Reynolds was safe, a friend. She squeezed his hand for a moment and shifted in the seat. "I must go in. Sunday morning is busy at our house and it's late."

"Just midnight, Sara. I thought we might talk a bit." He held tighter to her hand and then leaned closer, his mouth brushing the fine hair at her temple. "I've wanted to be with you for a long time, Sara. I'm not pushing you, but I want you to know that I'd like to see you. Spend time with you."

Remorse touched her and she lifted her face. She felt Tom's mouth touch her again and without thinking, reflexively, she moved back. The hesitation was imperceptible, but he felt it. The softness of her voice did nothing to cushion the message as she put an end to his hopes.

"I don't want to take up your time, Tom. You have so much to offer the right girl. But it isn't me."

His sigh was eloquent and with a shake of his head he released her and got out of the car. She was standing by the open door by the time he came around to let her out and she smiled at him. "Friends, Tom?"

"Sure, Sara. Friends."

It was a long night. She left her bed and stood by the window that looked out over the backyard. The temptation rose before her. Call him. Write to him. Marcie's letter had contained his address and phone number. It lay inside her top desk drawer and the thought of it there drew her.

The need to see him again had been urgent for four weeks, his face had haunted her dreams. The revelation that his touch gave her pleasure, that his hands and mouth had aroused her so easily was frightening. He was a stranger and she had melted against him. He had kissed her and held her, his hands had caressed her throat, had touched her hair and face. Without fear, she had allowed him access to her that boggled her mind as she considered her actions.

The breeze through the screened window was fresh, still damp with the evening dew. In the east the sun was still below the horizon, the air still cool as the sky began to color faintly with bands of pinkish grey. Later, by noon, she thought, it would be hot.

But now, in Sara's room, another source had begun to warm her. The memory of Cal Hyatt brought a flush to her cheeks, yearning enveloped her body when she traced her fingertips over the paths his had taken. Her basic honesty forced her to admit that she wanted to see him again even as she realized the futility of a long-range relationship. He was a busy man. His life was spent on a ranch, he had daily obligations, little free time. The sparse information he had volunteered had told her little, only that a holiday was rare in his life.

And yet she felt drawn, with a yearning that almost shamed her. Her cheeks felt warm and her fingertips touched the smooth skin as she closed her eyes and felt once more the heat of his opened mouth against her face.

Her eyes opened wide as she felt the curling excitement deep in her body. She wanted to see him again, she admitted to herself. No, more than that, she needed to see him. Her ponderings for the past weeks had brought her no peace. She had argued the pros and cons of contacting him over and over. And still, the bottom line was firm. He had stirred her senses, he had touched a part of her that had been sealed up and desolate. The need to see him, to know his touch again was all she could think about as she watched the slow sunrise.

With fingers that trembled, she sealed the envelope an hour later and stamped it. With the sound of church bells ringing in her ears, she detoured into the post office parking lot, pulled up in front of the drop box, and deposited her letter. The clang of the metal flap as it closed was final and she took a deep breath as she pulled onto the highway and headed for church.

_____ FOUR _____

When the telephone rang, just after two o'clock, Cameron O'Brien frowned. Sunday dinnertime was sacrosanct, ranking right up there with Sunday school and church services. Meals were usually casual affairs, with everyone on their own for breakfast and as many of his children at the table as were home at dinnertime. But midday on Sunday was family time and phone calls were an interruption he detested. Walking behind his chair as she headed for the kitchen, Sara slowed, her hand touching his shoulder for a moment. Without seeing his face, she felt the tenseness of his muscles and then he chuckled, receiving her silent message, his irritation bending to her serenity.

Jonathan rose, moving with an ease that belied his height and girth and headed for the hallway where the phone sat on a small table next to the stairway. "Hello." His greeting was clearly heard in the dining room. He paused a moment and then spoke again.

"Yes, she is." Sara's head turned and she listened intently. Surely, Tom had understood. She shook her head and stepped toward the hall. Jonathan met her at the doorway, a puzzled frown furrowing his brow. He raised an eyebrow and shrugged as she stood hesitantly before him.

"I don't know who it was, sis. He asked if Sara was here. I said you were and he thanked me nicely and hung up." Explanation over, Jonathan slid back into his chair and eyed the cake that graced his placemat. "You sure haven't lost your touch, have you, sis?" His grin was wide as he picked up his fork. The long table before him bore the remnants of Sara's Sunday dinner. Preparing it had always been a labor of love for her, rising early to begin cooking before church, hurrying home after the service to complete and serve the meal. Her brothers were not without gratitude.

"Sara makes the best chocolate cake in Goose Creek." Dennis's pronouncement lost some of its fervor, mumbled as it was through a mouthful. But his enthusiasm was unmistakable as he tackled his dessert.

"You make my day, Dennis. No one enjoys my cooking more than you do." Her hands full of dishes, Sara headed once more for the kitchen.

"Did you recognize him?" Patrick's low voice questioned Jonathan as Sara let the swinging door close behind her.

"It wasn't Tom, if that's who you have in mind, Pat. Wasn't anyone I know." Jonathan shrugged, dismissing his brother's worried look. "He'll probably call back."

In the kitchen, Sara stood before the sink, rinsing the plates she had gathered from the table, her mind working. Her thoughts were jumbled. It couldn't be Tom, she decided. Jonathan would have recognized him. What if . . . Impossible, I just mailed the letter this morning. I have Cal on the brain. She stacked the plates on the counter and reached for a towel. Drying her hands slowly and then tossing the terry towel over her shoulder, she passed through the swinging doors again.

Patrick was gathering up silverware and grinned at her teasingly. "If I clear up in here, may I be excused from dishes, ma'am?"

"Heavy date, Patrick?" Affection glowed from her eyes as she considered him. Tall, dark, and handsome . . . he was what every girl dreams of, she decided. Almost as tall and handsome as Callen Hyatt. The thought slipped into place and filled her mind. Go away, Cal, she thought with irritation. And was even more irritated as she felt the warmth flood her cheeks; warmth that thoughts of Cal produced with such ease. Her expressive face held a look that baffled Patrick as he watched her, and he wondered again what she was thinking. Sara held so much inside. He might never know who or what had made her so quiet and introspective over the past weeks. I need to spend some time with her, he thought. Maybe tonight when the house is quiet. In the meantime . . . his mind was wandering again, he realized, and a perfectly lovely date was on hold.

His blue eyes were innocent as he walked around the table, hands deftly gathering knives and forks as he went. "Uh, look, sis . . . Debbie and I are going to the beach and I told her I'd pick her up before three." He stood before Sara, hands full of silverware, an engaging grin in place that revealed deep dimples in both cheeks, and knew that he had won his case.

I can never resist him! The thought brought an answering smile into being and Sara shook her head ruefully. "Give it to me, Patrick! What good are you to me when you've got Debbie on the brain!"

"Thanks, sis. I owe you one!" He deposited his double handful on the table and turned to her. His familiar smile faded. "Didn't work out with Tom, did it?"

"No, Patrick, it didn't. I'm sorry."

With surprisingly gentle fingers, he ruffled her carefully pinned hair, tugging at a strand that curled in defiance. "I won't pull that again, Sara. Tom had the tickets and I thought . . . well, let's just say I had hopes."

Impulsively, she leaned forward and reached up to touch her lips to his cheek. "I love you and I appreciate your concern, Pat, but I'm a big girl now. I'll be fine."

"I want you to be happy, sis."

She hesitated and the words did not come easily to her, but her voice was firm as she spoke. "I'm happy, Patrick. I have a good life, a job I enjoy, and my family." Most of that is true, she told herself. If I'm not happy at least I'm not unhappy. Not really.

Thankfully, the sound of the doorbell took his attention and she stepped back. "Answer that, Patrick. And then be off with you. Don't get sunburned." She reached for a tray from the buffet and began loading it.

"I'll get the door." Dennis was on his way down the stairs as he spoke and Patrick turned toward the archway that led to the front foyer, watching as his brother opened the screen door. The low rumble of voices in the hallway moved closer and Sara looked over her shoulder, tray in hand.

A low sound drew Patrick's eyes to her face and he watched as her lips formed a name and then repeated it, softly, tenderly, and with a passion that surprised him.

"Cal . . ." She was barely conscious of her own whisper, hardly aware of the brothers who watched her with a mixture of apprehension and amazement. Her eyes were wide and startled, her mouth lifted in a gentle smile, and as she brushed past Patrick she deposited the tray in his hands, moving around him as if he were but a slight obstacle in her path.

Tall and silent, the man watched her. Wary, as if unsure of his welcome, his big hands fell loosely at his sides. And then she spoke again, carefully, as if the word were drawn from her by a force she could not deny.

"Cal . . ." Again it was a whisper and it brought a faint uptilting of his lips to the stern visage of the man who stood silently watching her. She halted before him and without changing expression he reached for her, the calloused fingers gripping hers, tugging her closer, until she felt the brush of his clothing against her dress. Then he spoke, and the words were what she had waited for during the long month that had seemed to last a lifetime.

"I had to come, Sara. I had to see you again." His voice was as she had remembered it during the lonely night hours: soft with an underlying strength, deep, resonant, the bass tones a rumble in his chest.

As if frozen in place, she watched him and her eyes moved slowly over the harsh lines of his face. Surely, he couldn't look so strong, so handsome, so right. Surely, her memory had amplified his sheer masculine perfection, from the heavy brows to the determined chin. From the eyes that watched her and held her captive to the firm mouth that had given her moments of unforgettable pleasure. She inhaled audibly as Patrick's hand upon her shoulder broke her concentration. Her head swung around toward him and the dazed look in her eyes frightened him.

"Sara, do you think you could introduce us to

your . . . friend?'' His hesitation was deliberate and Sara released one of Cal's hands to turn to her brother.

"I'm sorry, Patrick. I didn't mean to be rude." Breathless and wispy, her voice betrayed her uncertainty and surprise. And then the hand that gripped hers squeezed harder, reassuringly, before Cal released her only to slip his arm around her waist; the solid warmth of his palm resting against her ribs until she felt the support of his body, hard and firm against her. Awareness of the lean-muscled frame that offered her support brought quick color again to her face and her confused introductions were hasty.

"This is Cal . . . Callen Hyatt. I met him in New York . . .''

A sound that could only be described as a growl issued from Patrick's throat. "You haven't mentioned him.'' His narrowed eyes collided with clear, blue pupils that had just moments before been fastened on his sister. The arrival of Jonathan from the living room completed the trio and Cal faced the O'Brien brothers without hesitation. Three pairs of eyes challenged him now. Three faces that were somber and stern as they considered him, faces that were masculine copies of the beauty that had haunted him for a month.

He released Sara and stepped in front of her, offering his hand to Patrick. Fingers touched and then palms met. Patrick nodded shortly. "This is Dennis, Jonathan there, and I'm Patrick. Sara's brothers.''

"I would have known that without being told.'' The husky voice replied and Cal allowed his eyes to meet each of the three men who faced him, giving them time to assess him silently. His left hand touched Sara with silent assurance and her fingers twined with his gently. Her head was spinning, her cheeks were flushed, and her breath caught in her throat. In a few short minutes, her world had changed. Cal was here, real, solid, and determined.

"I met your sister in New York and she made quite an impression." His explanation was simple and Patrick nodded.

"Obviously. But what took you so long to get back to her?"

"Patrick!" Sara moved forward, embarrassed at the blunt question.

"It's all right, Sara . . ." The light in his eyes was tender as Cal glanced down at her. "Your brother has a right to ask me questions."

"No, he hasn't." She lifted her head and glared at the semi-circle of protectors that Cal faced. "I'm a big girl now. Cal is here to see me and I'd like to speak to him for a moment." With a look that threatened certain retribution, she stood her ground. Without speaking, the brothers consulted and as Patrick nodded their decision, Sara backed toward the screen door.

Surprisingly acquiescent, Cal followed her as they escaped to the relative privacy of the front porch.

"I must ask you to ignore my brothers, Cal. They tend to hover over me." Her fingers moved restlessly against her skirt, hiding among the folds, and her heart began an erratic tattoo that brought color to her cheeks.

His eyes assessed her, sweeping from the curls that would not be contained by the severity of her hairstyle, down to the pulse that fluttered in her throat, then touching briefly and tenderly on the rise of her breasts. He watched her fingers mesh tightly at her waist as she became conscious of his scrutiny and he smiled with gentle understanding. She was nervous, aware, afraid, and he would not have it. His fingers covered her hands, long, brown, and calloused against her paler flesh.

"Don't be afraid of me, Sara. Never be afraid." His other hand found the hollow of her back and he drew her closer, until she felt the heat of his body through her clothing. He lifted her hands and placed them on his chest where they rested uneasily. And then his fingertip touched her chin and lifted her face, waiting until she raised her eyes before he spoke.

"I didn't want to rush you, Sara. I'd like to court you, take my time with you, but I can't. I've come to get you. I want to take you home with me."

With a sigh that spoke of surrender, a smile that bestowed upon him the promise of her passion, she gave him her answer. Her confusion was gone, her fear of the unknown calmed by the honest emotion he showed her. The restless nights, the lonely days were no more. Without knowing what she sought, her search was at an end. The strength of Cal Hyatt drew her, the knowledge that he wanted her gave her assurance and the hands that had curled against his chest moved to his face, fingers touching the lines and creases, becoming bold as they explored. Without courtship, without knowing any more about him than what two hours' time in New York had told her, she found what she had been looking for in the strong, stern face of Callen Hyatt.

"Yes." The single, hesitant word was what he had waited for and with gentle deliberation his mouth sought hers, his lips began a tender caress that hinted of passion to come, asking only that she return the soft pressure of his mouth, making no demands, receiving her whispered acceptance, and sealing their agreement. His head lifted and she met his look with green eyes that shimmered. Tears sparkled and she blinked, unwilling to let them fall. Can I love him so soon? The question and answer were as one. Yes . . . yes . . . the quiet joy washed over her and her radiance assured him. A grin split his face and with a laugh that vibrated his chest, Cal celebrated his victory.

She would never be able to remember the events of that day in sequence. A blur of tall men, scattered around the living room, low voices exchanging information, a pair of eyes that followed her as she moved about the room. The dining room table with chairs tipped back as numerous cups of coffee were consumed, the cake plate empty, a few crumbs scattered across the tablecloth, and beneath it all the knowledge that Cal had not forgotten her. That he had come for her.

The evening passed in a series of conversations, her father's face serious as he spoke alone with Callen Hyatt, his questions basic and blunt. The answers he received caused him to nod thoughtfully, his brow furrowed as he listened carefully to the tall man who had come to claim his daughter. The fact of his coming was enough of a surprise to jolt the household. His intent had the effect of an earthquake on the four O'Brien men. Cal Hyatt wanted Sara. He wanted her now and he wanted her in Florida. He was polite, open with his answers and information. he brought names and phone numbers of men who would attest to his good name and reputation. He came well prepared, thought Cameron. He doesn't have any time to waste and he doesn't plan on taking no for an answer.

And then there was Sara. His daughter, the sparkle that brightened his mornings, the serene power that held his household together, the calm beauty that refreshed his tired eyes every evening at the dinner table. She stood behind the couch quietly, her fingers just inches from the broad shoulders of Cal, her eyes lowered, her expressive mouth half smiling, and he saw a gentle shudder wash over her slender form. For just a moment her eyes closed and then the heavy lids lifted and she looked full into his face. A smile of infinite surety lit her countenance and she lifted her fingers slowly, moving them just inches until they rested lightly on the shoulders of the man who had come to claim her. Without looking around, quietly accepting her presence, he reached up, his open palm swallowing her hand, touching her gently, his attention still fully on her father.

With a tired smile, Cameron rose to his feet. And without hesitation Cal stood to face him, Sara's hands slipping from him to clasp lightly at her waist. A hand that had done manual labor for over forty years, fingers thickened and bent, tough and strong, reached out and his breath caught as Cal recognized acceptance. Stooped shoulders straightened a bit as the elder O'Brien sighed, the sound piercing Sara to the quick. It was the echo of his loss and she felt his hurt even as she silently rejoiced in his acceptance of her choice. Cal was gracious in victory, his eyes warm with respect as he took the hand of Sara's father.

"Take care of my daughter, Cal. She's worth more than life to me." His voice was rough with emotion, but Cameron O'Brien looked at the man before him with a quiet threat in his gaze.

"Yes, sir, I know that." The respect was real. Cal had come to sense the hard core of strength that Sara's father had built his life upon. His family was of prime importance, their well-being was his first concern. His daughter's happiness was vital and woe be unto the man who harmed her in any way. "I intend to give her a good life." He glanced at Sara and the look spoke volumes. "I've waited a long time to find a wife. I knew after one evening in New York with your daughter that she was unusual. During the past month I've been unable to concentrate on much else.'' He grinned and the two men shared his meaning with an exchange of flashing eyes. ''Thank you, sir.''

With an audience that watched them closely, Cal reached for Sara's hand and drew her behind him toward the foyer and then out through the door. He barely paused on the front porch, towing her silently across the grass until they reached the relative privacy of a huge oak tree at the side of the house.

The shadows were deep beneath the low branches, the sun had long ago set and the night sounds were all around them. Without speaking a word, he drew her into the shelter of his arms and pressed her warm body against his, a soft groan whispering into the strands of her hair as he held her closely,. She felt the beat of his heart, hard and measured, against her cheek, the faint abrasion of his fingertips as he touched her cheek with one hand and then felt her chin rest against his palm as he tipped her head back.

The angle of his jaw and cheekbones were softened in the darkness and his eyes were shadowed. She sought for a hint of his thoughts in the somber visage that beheld her, but before she could penetrate the dim light his head bent to her and his mouth took possession of hers. A gentle kiss that was in direct contrast to his desperate hold on her body, a tender caress that touched her lips with careful deliberation and then moved on to taste the smoothness of her throat. She felt the shiver of response begin and tried in vain to control it. Her body sagged against him and she drew a breath, whispering his name without thought.

''Cal . . .'' The sound held a thread of fright that was not lost on him as it penetrated his concentration. She smelled so sweet, her body was so yielding against his, her mouth so soft. And then he realized that he had frightened her and he drew back, his hands releasing her to soothe and ease her away from his nearness.

"I'm sorry, Sara. I didn't mean to jump on you that way. I just couldn't stand it another minute without touching you." They were separated by inches of space and she felt the strength flow back into her body, released from his closeness.

"Cal . . ." Again, the sound of his name whispered from her lips and he smiled in the darkness. Would he ever tire of her calling his name? "I feel like I've been run over by a steamroller, Cal." She shook her head and stepped back another few inches, but he followed her, aware of his effect on her.

"I should have done this differently, Sara. I know that. But when I walked into your house and saw you I couldn't think of anything else except taking you home with me. All the way up here, the closer I got, the more I realized that I wanted to marry you and take you back to the ranch. It didn't occur to me that you might not feel the same way." He reached to touch her hair and his fingers twined in its darkness, the curls soft in his hand. "I knew in New York that you were special, different. And when you left without giving me a chance to call you or see you again, I was upset." He grunted and his anger was just beneath the surface. "Marcie refused to give me your address or phone number and I went home and pouted. I was determined to forget you. I decided you were too soft for ranch life, you probably wouldn't like horses, and I was better off without seeing you again."

His brief laugh mocked his own foolishness. "I was wrong, so wrong, little girl." He slid his hand to her shoulder and his grip tightened suddenly. "Yesterday, I finally realized that I had to see you again. If you hadn't been glad to see me, if you hadn't smiled at me and looked at me the way you did, I don't know what I would have done." With a short, harsh snort of derision, he answered his own question. "Probably thrown you over my shoulder and tried to leave. Not that I'd have had any chance with those three football players you live with!"

Her voice was teasing and soft. "They don't play football any more. They haven't since high school. They are kind of protective, aren't they?"

"I'm glad." Solemn words that approved of her sheltered existence. His hand moved to her arm and then to her hand, separating her fingers and tracing them with his own. "I haven't asked you, have I?"

She shook her head and he lifted her fingers to his mouth as he spoke again. "Will you marry me, Sara? Will you come back home with me and be my wife?" Her head moved again, but this time in a slow up and down motion and she reached up to touch him, her other hand coming to rest on the side of his face, fingers tracing his hairline.

"I mailed a letter this morning, Cal. It will be waiting for you when you get back to Florida. We can read it together."

With a sound that was a blend of satisfaction and desire, he turned his face to kiss her palm as she touched him. His lips moved softly against the warmth of her hand and his tongue followed the crease of her thumb as it rested against his cheek.

"Cal!" This time his name was spoken in a softly shocked manner that brought a look of anticipation to his face.

"It will be fun teaching you about life and love, little girl." The gentle teasing in his tones soothed her flustered feelings and she laughed softly as she rescued her hands and tucked them into her pockets.

"How long will we . . . how long before . . . ?" She hesitated a moment, her words unsure. His smile broadened, understanding her unspoken questions.

"We'll be here as long as it takes to get a license and find a preacher, Sara. You can start packing tomorrow morning while I find out about the legalities. If I can cut red tape, I will."

"I've never wanted a big church wedding, Cal. I'm not interested in bridesmaids and all that, but my dad will expect us to be married in the church."

"Is that what you want, Sara? If it is, it's all right with me. I'll do anything I have to in order to make it legal and head for home." He straightened and she was surprised again at his size and build. Her memory had bathed him in a golden glow until she was sure that he couldn't possibly be nearly as large and handsome as she remembered. But the real man more than measured up to her dreams: tall and broad in the shoulders, narrow waisted with legs that were longer than any she had ever seen before. With his boots on, he stood taller than any of her brothers and Dennis was several inches over six feet tall. She measured her own slender build against him and felt overwhelmed for a moment. He could crush her without much effort at all. His size, his obvious physical strength, his muscular build were enormous when she compared it with her own fragility.

A smile traced her lips as she leaned her head against the solid wall of his chest and felt his arms enclose her once more. Safe, secure, cherished . . . his embrace was a fortress, a bulwark about her.

Above her, Cal smiled. A look of deep satisfaction spoke silently of his pleasure in Sara, his pride in her quiet gentility, her total suitability for the role he had offered her. He vowed to be careful with her, gentle, understanding of her youth and innocence. It was difficult to wait, but with a woman like Sara, it was worth it. He would take her home as his bride and begin their life together on the ranch that was his heritage. His arms tightened about her in anticipation of the time of her awakening and his own fulfillment of a dream.

FIVE

Silver edged the rim of a cloud that hung over the trees along the driveway and even as she watched, the moon made its appearance once more, rising slowly as it lent its reflected glow to the night. She had watched the stars, noted the gathering clouds that began obscuring the clear sky, and then waited patiently while the full moon vanished for a while behind a fast moving harbinger of the storm that hovered in the west.

The wind was rising, swirling dust and a few leaves in the driveway. The heat lingered, a reminder of the Florida sun that had beat down unmercifully all day. Sara lifted her face to catch the dusty scent of showers in the air. A scent that promised relief to the pasture land, wilting in the early summer heat, without rain for well over a week. Gently, the pale illumination touched her face and the traces of tears that had washed her eyes and left silver streaks on her cheeks glowed faintly in the moonlight.

The man behind her watched silently from the huge bed, his fingers clasped behind his head, eyelids half-lowered as he assessed the slender figure that stood outlined against the window. A cotton gown covered her body, leaving only feet and ankles exposed, bare and strangely vulnerable. The rounded, curved profile revealed a shadowy form, faintly visible and suddenly tempting. He shifted, turning to his side and watched her as the rustle of the sheets made her aware of him; watched her stiffen and then turn her back to him.

"Sara." Her name hung in the air and he felt her response as she lifted her head a bit more and straightened as if to raise a barrier between them. "Shall I come get you?" She heard the unspoken threat in his quiet words and relented.

"That won't be necessary, Cal." His keen ears caught the muffled sob she tried to swallow as she spoke and again he shifted, this time to rise on one elbow as he watched her turn and take the few steps that brought her to the bedside. She sat on the edge of the mattress and slipped her feet beneath the sheet before she lay back on the plump feather pillow that still bore the faint depression where her head had lain earlier. Her eyes closed wearily and she tugged the sheet up to her armpits before she folded her arms across her breasts.

But he would not let her escape so easily and his whisper breathed against her as he leaned over her.

"Look at me, Sara." His fingers touched her face, following the path of her tears and with an involuntary jerk she turned from him. It was a small matter, easily solved. And with hands that held her firmly, gently but implacably, he turned her once more to face him. Her head fell back and her eyes opened, obediently fastened on his face as he covered her with the weight of his lower body, pressing her into the mattress. His fingers slipped upward on her arms until he clasped her narrow shoulders. And then, he bent to her and she watched as the shadowed features came nearer. Inches away, he paused and his eyes swept over her face, dimly revealed in the glow from the window.

There was silence between them, but the stillness was alive with the memory of the passion they had shared. With searching eyes, she noted his frown, the lines that creased his cheeks, each small wrinkle that edged the outer corner of his eyes. She knew that face, had traced her own fingers over each rugged inch, had brushed countless feathery kisses across his jaw. With the tip of her tongue, she had closed his dark eyes, bravely experimenting with loveplay so new that she was unsure of her own ability to please him with her caresses. And he had been pleased. As surely as she recognized her own degree of pleasure, she knew she had given him satisfaction—until the moment of their joining. Until his seeking and finding had told him that she was not what he had expected. Until he had found release in her slender body. And then, as his breathing eased and he was able to speak again, he had shattered her quiet joy with his faintly accusing words.

"You weren't a virgin, were you." It wasn't a question but a statement of fact and she felt shamed as she moved restlessly beneath his weight.

Her whisper was so low he almost missed it. "I never said I was, Cal."

His arms straightened and he loomed over her, lips compressed and unsmiling. "No, you didn't, did you. And I didn't ask, either. I just assumed." He sat up beside her suddenly and shrugged. "No matter . . ."

But it had mattered, obviously a great deal. She saw the same unsmiling expression now as he lowered his mouth the scant inches it took until he made contact and she felt the cool pressure of his lips as he kissed her. Not the heat of his earlier embrace, the fevered, bruising, open-mouthed kisses that had driven her beyond control. Hot, wet caresses that had introduced her to the realm of his passion and taken her on a breathtaking path that had led to the full awakening of her senses; until she had been filled and overwhelmed by the beauty of his mouth and hands and body and had responded with unrestrained joy. She felt the hot blush that seared her throat and face as she recalled her whimpers and cries of fulfillment and his mouth was cool against her cheek as he spoke again.

"I didn't mean to make you unhappy, Sara. I spoke before I thought, earlier . . . you took me by surprise. I expected . . . well you know what I expected, but it's not important now."

He shifted again, lifting her, easing the gown from her body. Her lips opened to protest and his mouth was there, tasting vaguely like the scent of her own body. And then his lips covered hers and she tasted again the heated flavor of his desire that made her think of spices and pomegranates and all things exotic and forbidden. His hands were moving against her skin, dark against the fairness of her breasts and she shivered, her eyes closing as she tried to fight the sensations that once more threatened her control.

"Don't, Cal . . . I don't want you to . . ." But her words were lost as his mouth opened against hers and her whispers turned to tiny cries of yearning and need as he overcame her protests and brought her swiftly to a shattering climax with knowing, clever fingers and hot, wet kisses that soothed even as they inflamed her flesh. She felt his weight against her and with involuntary movements, she lifted and shifted. She accepted him, entwining her legs and arms with his, until they were a single shadow in the moonlight, straining together, seeking the ultimate peak of pleasure two humans can know.

She glanced into the bathroom mirror and sighed, grateful for small things. Like finding herself alone in bed this morning, like having a bathroom within the master bedroom. Like being able to locate and slip into her gown before she rose, before she sought the privacy of the bathroom she had barely noticed last night.

Now the harsh sunlight bathed her, reflecting through the uncurtained window and in its glare, she felt exposed and naked. But the mirror was kind and she smiled faintly as she surveyed herself, thankful that the hours of early morning had brought sleep and soothed the lines of unhappiness that had marred her face in the moonlight. She looked pale but serene and with careful fingers she traced the faint shadows under her eyes, pleased that her silent tears had left so little trace to remind her of the vigil she had kept in the moonlight. She splashed water against her cheeks, ran wet fingers through her hair, and then lifted her head to meet the eyes of her husband in the mirror as he stood in the bathroom doorway behind her.

"Good morning, sleepyhead. I brought you coffee and Bess is keeping your breakfast warm." His lips curved in a smile that was meant to reassure her, but she saw instead the cool measuring glance his eyes gave her and a chill destroyed the faint warmth of her mood.

"Thanks, Cal. I'll be right down, as soon as I find something to wear." She turned to face him and her own smile was strained, her eyes not quite meeting his as she brushed past him into the bedroom. Her fingers were busy, pulling shorts and a knit top from the drawer where Bess had deposited her folded clothing late last evening. A quick search through two other drawers revealed her underwear and she turned to face him, bra and panties in hand. Her lip caught for a moment between her teeth and her eyes sought for understanding. But with his arms crossed and his hip leaning against the doorjamb, he looked immovable, watching her with a cool half-smile that brought a quick blush to her face.

"Maybe I'll just wait here for you," he murmured and then at her flustered look, he relented and stood erect, his hands sliding into his pockets as he moved toward the door. "I'll be in the kitchen, Sara."

She sighed with relief. The events of yesterday were all too new, too recent and she had barely become used to the weight of his ring on her finger. It would take more than a day before she could accustom herself to sharing a bedroom with him—let alone a bathroom. Her clothing went on with ease. Familiar fabrics, scented with the spicy sachet from her dresser drawers at home, were comforting in this place where she was the stranger.

The hallway was silent, the stairs creaked faintly as she ran quickly down the carpeted treads, and then she heard the hushed laughter and muted voices from the kitchen at the back of the house. She slipped in the swinging door and deposited her half-empty coffee cup on the table, pulling out a chair and easing her way into the sudden pause in conversation.

"Good morning, Bess. I'm sorry I'm so late." Her eyes met those of the woman who stood by the stove, a smile still curving her lips as she glanced from one to the other of the couple who sat at her kitchen table.

"That's all right, missus. I've saved you some pancakes and eggs, but I'm afraid Cal here ate most of the bacon." She bent to the oven and with a red-checked potholder pulled out a plate, covered with an inverted metal pie tin, which she removed as she lowered Sara's breakfast to the table before her.

"Oh, thanks, Bess. This is fine. In fact, much more than I'm used to." She looked up at Cal who shrugged his shoulders and raised an eyebrow.

"She expects everyone to eat a big breakfast, Sara. Dig in and do the best you can with it." He was nursing the last of his coffee, the mug tipping to drain as he tilted his head back.

She watched as his throat moved, the muscles visible beneath his skin, and then his hand wiped a trace of liquid from his upper lip and her eyes followed the brushing of his fingers. She was caught up in him, in the graceful, masculine movements of his hands, of the strong length of his fingers, the fair, crisp curls that covered his forearms beneath folded-back shirt sleeves. His hands, the fingers that had touched her in the night . . . the thought brought warmth rushing through her. Like the west wind that had blown through their bedroom window, cooling their heated flesh as they listened to the rain that swept over the treetops. Moisture that dampened down the dust and refreshed the grass . . . swept by the breeze that billowed the sheer curtains at the window.

She blinked, feeling foolish in the ranch house kitchen, daydreaming while Cal headed for the back door and Bess turned toward the dishwasher with his coffee mug. At the door, he paused and glanced at the girl who watched him, noting the faint shadows under green eyes that had enchanted him so easily in New York. That still enchanted him if the truth be known, even though that enchantment was tinged with a faint cynical regret. She had fooled him, perhaps not purposely, but in her young, charming way, she had made him believe in her purity, her innocence. He watched as the green eyes darkened, confused at his scrutiny and without speaking, he left the house, letting the screen door slam behind him.

It was the work of less than an hour to straighten their bedroom, wipe the bathroom sink, and rearrange her clothing in the large closet that held Cal's things in one side, leaving her with over half of the rod to fill. She savored the sight of her dresses and blouses hanging next to his shirts, her small shoes and boots on the floor, side by side with his black dress shoes and two pairs of tooled-leather boots. A pair of scuffed deck shoes were piled in one corner and she pulled them into line with the rest of his shoes, feeling a thrill of possession as she handled his belongings.

She caught up a hanger from the rod and held the western-style shirt before her. Recent memories made it easy to picture Cal inside the limp fabric, his muscular chest filling out the material, the snaps taut against his flesh. And with a sudden move, she clasped it to her breasts and buried her face in it, imagining for a moment that she could catch a trace of his scent in the freshly laundered smell.

"I'll be a good wife, Cal . . . I promise . . ." Her lips whispered the words and her eyes filled with tears as she hung the shirt back on the rod. The knowledge that she had disappointed him was bitter and she swallowed the bile that rose in her throat.

"I should have told him, I should have let him know that I wasn't a virgin." Her whispered regrets bore the echoes of the tears she refused to shed. And her thoughts were filled with the sadness that this morning had brought to her heart.

". . . oh, Cal, you were really the first. The other time was so long ago. I can almost forget it." But she knew she would never forget the pain, the bruises she had hidden for days, the fright of not knowing if she would find herself pregnant.

And then the memory of the past overwhelmed her again. The shame of being so gullible, of believing and trusting a friend, of recognizing too late that her date had been slipping out to the parking lot to share a bottle with his buddies. And then the moment on a quiet country road, when her cries for help had gone unanswered and she had suffered the humiliation of being stripped of her panties and feeling the suffocating weight of Jay Whitney as he pawed and thrust at her. For a moment she was once more that frightened girl, sobbing in the corner of the front seat while he sobered up, listening to his retching and groaning as he stood outside the car, leaning to vomit in the road before he took her home.

Home, where he patted her arm and once more muttered a brief apology for losing his head. He had lost his head, she thought ruefully, but I lost much more. She thought of the months and years that she withdrew from the young men who had been her high-school dates, until finally they had left her alone. She withdrew from casual, friendly gestures, recognizing that she couldn't stand to have men near her. That other than her brothers and her father, she didn't want to be touched by anyone.

Until that night in New York, when Cal had so easily broken down her barriers. When his warmth and charm had awoken a response in her that brought to life the sensual, womanly part of her that had lain dormant for so long.

She didn't believe in love at first sight. She had never believed in fairy tales. But Cal had struck a chord, had touched her with gentle hands, had shown her the promise of her own passion and then had left her with an empty, aching place inside that would not be filled by anything or anyone else but him.

She sat on the edge of the bed she had shared with her husband last night and faced the truth. The awakening of her love in the moment when Cal had announced his intention to take her back home with him had been astonishing to her. But now, in the hard light of day, she realized that it was a onesided emotion. Cal wanted her, he needed a wife. His dreams for the future included a family.

He had spent almost six hours in the car with her yesterday after the early morning wedding, answering her questions, telling her about his ranch, describing the property, the house, his housekeeper; and finally had asked her if she shared his dream of a family. She had nodded, agreeing to his every suggestion, dazed by the handsome stranger who had taken over her life. Taken over her life, her heart, her body.

She closed her eyes, conjuring up visions of the hours they had spent in this bed last night. Her green eyes misted with forlorn tears as she recalled the words he had spoken. "You weren't a virgin, were you?" I'm not what he expected, she thought. I should have told him . . . but then he might not have wanted me. And he did want me, he said I was lovely . . . He said . . . she flushed as she recalled descriptive phrases he had used, broken phrases that promised pleasure, that praised her beauty. He desired her—that much she was sure of. He had said so, more than once.

The problem this morning was within herself. She had given her love to a man who was disappointed in his bride. She rose from the bed, automatically turning to smooth the wrinkles from the white spread before she headed for the bedroom door. I'll make the best of it, she vowed, her fingers moving to turn the knob. I'll make him love me, I'll love him enough for both of us.

Her narrow shoulders straightened as she passed through the hallway, but the smile that touched her lips was more wistful than happy as she ran down the stairway and headed for the kitchen.

The clouds gathered moisture and spilled it on the dry pasture land for several days. The dust no longer swirled with every wispy breeze that blew. The meadow was rich with greenery and the air was clean and fresh.

During the day, the sun was still hot, but the nights were cooler and the breeze that wafted through their bedroom windows touched their warm bodies with refreshing fingers.

The nights were a revelation to Sara. Desire and passion had been words without meaning, without substance. Up until now. No matter that Cal was almost a stranger to her during daylight hours. When darkness fell, when their bedroom door closed out the world, he became the husband she had only dared to dream of. With patience and gentle amusement, he wooed her. With barely restrained hunger, he led her, coaxing her with whispered words of praise, inviting her to partake in the pleasure they created. He filled their nights with warmth and tenderness and her heart with a gradual awakening.

During the day Sara saw Cal in snatches, usually for a few minutes while he drank coffee in the kitchen in lieu of breakfast. Most days he and his hands came in for a quick lunch, eaten silently and hurriedly. He sat at his desk for an hour or so each evening and then watched the evening news on television before bedtime. Sara decided that he just wasn't much for conversation, and she waited and watched him patiently . . . hoping for a warmth in their daytime relationship that seemed to be slow in developing.

Mornings were spent helping Bess wherever she could. She dusted and swept the never ending, sifting residue that permeated the doors and windows. In the afternoons, she shared the kitchen with Bess, venturing to suggest menu ideas and helping with cooking chores.

"You're not what I expected, you know," Bess observed. Her hands were full of dirty silverware and she rinsed it under the hot, running water before she loaded it into the dishwasher.

Sara turned from the refrigerator and closed the door. "What were you expecting, Bess?" She sat down gingerly on the edge of a chair and waited, as if the judgment of the older woman was of utmost importance. She was aware of the relationship between Cal and his housekeeper. She knew of the respect and unspoken love they shared. Such rapport could not be hidden from a casual observer, and Sara was more than casually interested in anything that had to do with her husband.

Bess turned to her and leaned against the sink countertop, folding her arms across her bosom and allowing a teasing smile to lift her lips in an easy grin. "Well, when he came back from New York, he was in a state. So, I figured he'd met a big-city gal who had him tied in knots." She raised her eyebrows mockingly at the girl who watched her so eagerly. "Then he left here in a flying hurry one day and brought you home with him. When you got out of that car out back, I quit worrying."

"Why? What made you change your mind?" Sara leaned forward, her eyes focused on Bess, as if she could prompt her to continue.

"Rest easy, girl." Bess closed the distance between

them and sat across the table, breathing a sigh as she eased herself into the chair. Sara scooted her own wooden chair around until she faced the friendly face that watched her closely.

Bess shook her head at the solemn expression Sara wore. "Cheer up, Sara. You and me are going to do real well together." She shifted and reached to pat roughly at the slender hand that lay with fingers clenched on the blue-and-white tablecloth. "You're all uptight, girl. Being a ranch wife takes time, you know. But, you'll do it, honey. I knew that first night that you were a long way from being sophisticated." Her drawling treatment of the word gave it a different meaning than Sara had ever connected it with. She laughed at the sour look Bess wore as she mocked the glamour of city life.

"You're right about that," she said, agreeing with a nod. "Life in Goose Creek was about as far from sophistication as you can get."

"Don't get me wrong, now." Bess was quick to make herself clear. "You're a fine young woman. You've had a good upbringing. I can see that, the way you bustle around here and pitch in to help." She looked intently across the table. "Do you miss your folks, Sara?"

Her fingers clasped instinctively as Sara felt a twinge of pain, somewhere in the region of her heart. "Sure, I do, Bess . . . sometimes a lot. And I've only been here just over a week." She leaned over the table and spoke softly. "Would you believe that my brothers and my father spoiled me terribly?"

"Nope!" Without hesitation the answer was given. "Maybe they took care of you. You know, kind of watched out for you. But you're a long way from being spoiled." As if she pronounced the final judgment,

Bess slapped her hands flat on the table and then levered herself up, pushing the chair back across the floor. "Come on, girl, we've got vegetables to pick out in the garden and cobbler to make for dinner.

The daughter she had never had began to resemble Sara in Bess's thoughts. The mother she could scarcely remember began to take on the attributes of the gruff, taciturn housekeeper in Sara's memory.

And so the summer slipped away, the work in the fields and pastures never complete. Late dinners were a fact of life; the hands retreating to the bunkhouse, Cal eating silently and then spending hours in his study with his paperwork and record keeping most evenings. Sara watched for a sign of change in him and found none. He was tired when he came in and spoke little. She waited for the rare times when his hand touched her hair as he passed her at the door. But mostly his smile was distracted, his mood casual.

His thoughts were anything but. Casual did not describe Cal's feelings toward Sara. He was distracted by her. She filled his thoughts when they were apart. She was with him when he sought solitude in the pastures and gently rolling acres that he rode almost daily. Her smile, the soft scent of her hair and body, the textures of her skin . . . they wound tentacles about him that clung invisibly, but tenaciously.

She was a paradox. She gave the appearance of innocence. She was naive and endearingly unknowing. And yet . . . he'd found that same innocence to be a lie. She had been with another man . . . perhaps other men. No, he didn't want to believe that. Surely not more than one, or she would be more experienced. Perhaps her actions were a lie . . . perhaps she only pretended to be . . .

With a pain-filled cry of frustration, Cal looked up

at the sky as if he sought answers to his unspoken questions. The instinct for survival had been strong since the long ago days of LouAnn. The young man who had been wounded by the deceit of a thoughtless girl had developed into a man who was not willing to give second chances. Not to anyone. Especially not to a young woman who had represented herself as a virtuous female.

"I'll just watch her a while. See how she handles herself around the men." He spoke to the wind and the hayfield that he rode through, to the horse that obeyed his unspoken commands as he turned back to the ranch house. "But it won't keep me from enjoying her." His final pronouncement was accompanied by a grin that split his somber face as he considered the nights that stretched before him. "Beginning with tonight!" The thought propelled him and it was with surprise that Sara saw him approach the house an hour before dinner.

She met him on the porch. "Is something wrong, Cal?" Her voice was anxious and he felt an inclination to soothe her.

"No." He glanced at her and his look took a quick but complete inventory. "Just hungry." He held her eyes and was gratified to see the slow flush that crept over her face as she registered his meaning. He held the door open and followed her into the kitchen.

"I'm going to write some checks, Sara. When will dinner be ready?" Without stopping, he crossed the kitchen and Sara looked at Bess with lifted shoulders and raised eyebrows.

"We haven't been on too strict a schedule lately, Cal. How about in an hour?" She trailed behind him to the doorway and watched as his long legs carried his lean body toward the den. Her eyes were warm as she noted the snug fit of his jeans and shirt, the easy gait of his muscular legs, and the ridge at the back of his hairline where his Stetson had clung tightly.

"Fine." The word was as abrupt as the closing of the door between them and she turned back to the kitchen.

Sara went to bed early, tucked in with a book she had read before. Its familiar pages were somehow comforting as she waited for Cal. She heard his footsteps on the stairs and found herself watching the doorway. The sight of his rumpled hair and wrinkled shirt brought a smile of anticipation to her face and she watched as he stripped to his briefs, piling his discarded clothing into the hamper before he walked into the bathroom to take his shower.

The intimacies of marriage were becoming a vital part of her life. Within the privacy of their bedroom, she sensed a growing affinity between them and she yearned to nourish it until it would bloom into . . . what? Did she dare hope that he would someday love her? Anxious for a sign of softening on his part, she nevertheless tried to give him room, tried to be patient.

But in silence he undressed, in silence she watched him, and in silence he came to her, damp and cool, scented by the soap he used, by the unique male aroma that was his.

The restraints he imposed on their relationship during the day vanished in the darkness. His arms reached for her nightly and she came to him readily. In his loving, he broke the bonds of silence and he gave her the warmth of his approval as he told her of her beauty, of the pleasure she afforded him. He spoke her name in tones that pleased her and his caresses brought whispers of yearning and broken cries of fulfillment from her lips. With tenderness, he brought her to a knowledge of her own passion before he sought satisfaction in her eager body.

He was a considerate lover, thoughtful and thorough. And then he slept, touching her, but separate, withdrawn in spirit—the process almost coinciding with his physical withdrawal after their lovemaking. Lying awake beside him, she dredged up moments to reflect on, and the night hours were long as she pondered over the changes that had taken place.

Memories. Those of Cal as he was during the few short days in Goose Creek, before their wedding, were her favorite. He had been warm and loving, his eyes gentle and tender, his touch flooding her with happiness. She hugged the warmth to herself and waited patiently through the night hours for sleep to claim her, while Cal slept next to her, close but not touching.

Her eyes became shadowed and the faint roundness of her figure faded as a new slimness shaped her body. Bess observed her silently and was concerned, finally making excuses for Cal as she watched Sara's eyes follow her husband, surmising problems that Sara was unwilling or unable to cope with.

"Cal is working awfully hard, missus. He'll be easier to get on with after he gets the new calves branded and sorted out."

"He's just tired, Bess. I understand."

"Cal isn't usually so abrupt, Sara. He must have a lot on his mind." Her hand touched Sara's slender shoulder encouragingly, but her eyes were worried as she watched the young woman walk from the room. The joyous bride that had entered this house just weeks ago was gone and in her place was a quiet, saddened girl who only brightened when Cal deigned to smile or speak to her.

Bess frowned and turned back to the stove. Something had gone wrong. From the first morning she had sensed a coolness, a turning away, almost a barrier between the two. Not only that, Cal had become aloof lately with his housekeeper. She missed the easy chatter, the warm conversations that had marked their relationship. And Bess was without a solution.

"Sure can't solve it if I don't even know the problem!" It had been a bad morning all the way around, following a sleepless night as she felt the threatening discomfort of her gall bladder making itself known. She grumbled, her words abrupt and loud, punctuated by the slamming of cupboard doors as she put away the breakfast things.

Sara heard the muttering, the words lost and muffled by the swinging door, but she caught the mood of the older woman and shared it. Bess was tired this morning, she thought. But more than that, she was pale and a little cranky. Not like herself at all. And Sara felt a moment's shame as she realized that she had ignored the older woman's mood this morning. With quick steps she turned and went back to the kitchen, surprising Bess as she silently pushed through the swinging door. One work roughened hand was flattened against her stomach and the other was braced firmly against the countertop as Bess stood silently near the sink, her head bent and her eyes closed.

"Bess?" Sara flew across the kitchen floor, her own problems forgotten as she realized that Bess was in pain. Her lips were compressed as if she withheld sounds that might betray her misery. Bess straightened quickly as Sara reached for her and then slumped against the countertop as the pain returned with a twisting wrench.

"What is it, Bess? What's wrong?" Her eyes took in the bent form, the stifled moan, and Sara slipped one arm around Bess's waist, guiding her to a chair at the table. She slumped heavily, propping up her head with one hand as she spanned her waistline with the other forearm.

"I'll be all right in a minute." Her breath caught. "It's just a cramp." Sara knew panic. It flooded her and she fled to the back door.

Cal was gone, acres separated them. She was alone and Bess was in pain. Not for a minute did Sara believe in the protests that fell from Bess's mouth.

A groan spun her around and she caught her breath at the grimace that twisted the pale features of the older woman. She was in charge, she realized, and Bess was hurting. Cal was out of reach, the hands were with him and Bess was depending on her.

She knelt before the chair and touched Bess's face. Her skin was clammy and chilled. "Come on, Bess. Lie down on the couch for a bit. I'll get you a drink of water." She coaxed and cajoled as she helped the woman to her feet and guided her from the kitchen, through the hallway and into the living room.

Soft groans marked her breathing as Bess gave in to the pain that had finally seized her shortly after breakfast. She had hidden it as well as she could while Cal and Sara were in the kitchen, but anger at the betrayal of her sturdy body had brought about her tempermental cupboard door slamming. Now, with Sara's gentle encouragement, she was finally willing to lie down and give in to the fiery torture that was taking over her body.

"I think I need to take my pills, missus. They're in the pantry, top shelf." The words puffed out weakly as Bess turned to her side on the couch. Without speaking, Sara turned and fled to the kitchen. She ran the water for a few seconds until it was cool and then quickly filled a glass before she reached on tiptoes for the two small vials of medication that bore Bess's name.

Her brows gathered as she read the instructions and noted the dates on the bottles. Bess had been on medication for several weeks and hadn't mentioned that she was ill. "I should have been helping her more," Sara whispered as she checked the dosage and opened the containers. "I've been moping around here and feeling sorry for myself and didn't even realize that she was sick." She noted the name of the physician on the bottle and made a quick decision as she hurried back to the living room.

"Thank you, Sara." Bess leaned on one elbow and tipped her head back as she swallowed the pills Sara had shaken out into her palm. With a sigh that trembled on the brink of a sob, she lay back down and eyed Sara with determination. "I'll be fine in a few minutes. Don't worry about a thing." She closed her eyes with relief and tried to relax.

It took only a moment for Sara to cross the room and reach the table in the corner that held a telephone and the slim yellow phone book. Her fingers moved rapidly down the pages until she found the number she wanted and with a quick glance at Bess, she dialed.

The receptionist agreed readily that Bess needed to see the doctor and within seconds had instructed them to come into the office. Sara turned from the phone and faced Bess squarely, her hands on her hips, prepared for battle.

"Don't argue, Bess. You know you need to see the doctor." She softened as she saw the panic that appeared for a moment in the tired blue eyes. And then Sara found herself on her knees by the couch, her arm holding tightly to the sturdy body that was curled defensively against the pain that had taken up residence.

"Let me help you, Bess. Let's get you to the car and I'll take you into town." She bent her head to the graying hair and brushed a quick kiss of comfort. She lifted and coaxed while Bess struggled to sit up and then rise to her feet. Then she leaned heavily on Sara's shoulder. They shuffled slowly, managing to reach the hallway and from there to the front door, Sara grabbing up her purse from the hall table as she passed. A shadow fell across the floor, blocking the sunlight as they neared the screen door. Sara's eyes widened in surprise as she faced the man who stood on the porch. He was a study in perplexity as he watched the two women through the screen.

"Bess . . . are you all right?" As he spoke, he moved rapidly forward, opening the door and lifting the weight from Sara's slender shoulder. He supported her easily with his arm around her waist. And she leaned into him with a sigh, glad to accept the strength he offered.

"Not too hot right now, Mr. Cochrane." Her voice was weak and Sara was spurred by its sound to move forward past her unexpected assistant. She ran to the car that sat beyond the gate at the head of the long driveway.

Moving quickly, her feet barely touched the ground as she opened the wooden gate that kept the small animals from the kitchen garden; and then looked back expectantly at the man who followed her, matching his footsteps to Bess's slower ones.

Her green eyes glowed with appreciation. "Thank you so much. If you'll just help me get her in the car . . ." She smiled fleetingly at the tall man, unaware that he had managed to assess her slender figure and flying curls as she moved ahead of him. So, this was Cal Hyatt's new bride. No wonder he kept her hidden away, she was a beauty. His eyebrows lifted in silent appreciation even as he helped Bess into the car.

Four hands worked at the seat belt as Bess let her head lean back on the headrest, her hands clenched into fists in her lap and her teeth biting painfully into her lower lip as she fought the slicing pain that refused to give her any relief. Four eyes met in tacit understanding as the two strangers faced each other outside the car door.

"What can I do?" The offer was immediate and Sara was grateful.

"If you could find Cal and let him know that Bess is ill, I'd really appreciate it. I'm taking her into town to the doctor's office and I'm not sure just where he is. Cutting hay, I think." Her words were hurried and a bit breathless and her smile was uneasy as she made her request.

Without hesitation, Les Cochrane nodded and gripped her elbow as he ushered her around the front of the car, opening the driver's door and easing her down into the seat.

"I'll take care of it, Mrs. Hyatt. Go on and get Bess into town." He closed the car door and stepped back, raising one finger to the brim of his hat as she turned the key in the ignition. Sara's eyes expressed her thanks again as she shifted into first gear and glanced up at the tall rancher who had helped her so readily and capably. And then she was moving down the driveway, the dust billowing behind her as she headed for the blacktop road that led to town.

SIX

I've never felt quite so alone in my life, Sara decided. The view from the hospital waiting room was bleak at first sight and hadn't improved any during the past three hours.

She stood before the large expanse of glass and leaned her forehead to rest for a moment against the cool window. Her eyes closed and her whisper held a trace of desperation. "Where are you, Cal? I need you."

To the doctor who approached her, she resembled a very young girl, her hair caught up in a ponytail, her slender form tucked into jeans and a soft knit shirt that clung to her youthful body.

And so his greeting was a question. "Mrs. Hyatt?"

Sara spun from the window and her eyes widened at his approach, uneasy as she scanned his somber face. "Yes, I'm Sara Hyatt."

Her hand thrust forward and was taken hold of in a friendly manner by the man who greeted her.

"I had hoped to meet you under better circumstances, Mrs. Hyatt." Dr. Richmond's words brought

94

a flutter of panic to join the butterflies that had been flourishing in Sara's stomach for the past hours.

"Is Bess going to be all right?" She looked defenseless and frightened, and the family doctor who had cared for half the town for the past thirty years decided that Cal had indeed married an innocent child. Holding her by the hand that rested in his, he led her to the vinyl-covered couch that sat against the wall.

"Sit down, Mrs. Hyatt."

"Sara, please . . ." she interrupted softly.

"All right . . . Sara." He dropped down beside her and continued. "Bess should have had this surgery weeks ago, without the trauma of an attack complicating things. But then, she never was very good at listening to advice." He leaned back on the stiff couch, trying to ease the ache that came from over two hours in surgery, stretching his long legs out before him. Then he relaxed and slouched next to her, as if he must take advantage of every opportunity that presented itself to gain a few minutes breathing space.

"But, is she all right?" she asked again. The question had been on the tip of Sara's tongue ever since the doctor had appeared and she was impatient for his reply.

He nodded briefly and his eyes made a measured survey of her as he slid upright on the cushion, one long arm moving to lie on top of the back of the couch so he was turned toward her. Cal Hyatt had picked a winner, that was sure. She wasn't nearly as young as he had first thought. But small, lots of dark curls hanging from the back of her head and the prettiest green eyes he'd ever seen.

His quick grin was welcome to Sara, and she visibly relaxed.

"She's not all right yet, Sara, but she will be." He

glanced out into the hallway and back to her. "Where's Cal? I thought he'd be here."

"A neighbor rode out to find him and send him in when I left with Bess. I thought he'd have been here by now, too." Her own eyes flicked uneasily to the archway that led to the nursing station and down the hall to the surgical suite. As if conjuring up a vision, she glanced again and smiled in relief as the tall figure of her husband came into sight.

She met him halfway, her hands going out in appeal and he slid his arms around her as he looked over her head into the face of Sam Richmond. "Is Bess . . ."

"She'll be fine, Cal. I just told your wife that that housekeeper of yours doesn't know how to take advice. Weeks ago, I emphasized that she needed to have that gall bladder out, but she wouldn't listen. Now, she'll pay the price." The doctor stood and stretched, and then his long body settled into the wrinkled green suit he had worn in surgery. "Those stones caused a lot of irritation and she's going to have a drainage tube in the incision for a few days. I don't see her going home for a week or so. Then we'll see how fast she gets back on her feet."

His eyes flicked to the woman Cal still held in his arms. "Your missus may be carrying a heavy load for a while, unless you can find another cook in the meantime."

Sara's head rose from the cradle it had found against Cal's heartbeat and she stiffened against him. Releasing herself from the arms that felt so welcome, she turned to face the doctor. "I'll be fine, doctor. I can handle the work without any trouble. Just get Bess well and back to us safely." Her soft voice was stronger now; now that she knew Bess would recover.

The ride into town had seemed to take forever, Bess

groaning in ever-increasing pain beside her as she half lay against the door of the truck. Sara had driven as fast as she could, thankful for the light traffic on the two-lane road that led into town. The sounds of discomfort from the woman beside her changed Sara's plans as the large sign at the edge of town, directing her to the hospital, sent her in that direction. From the looks of Bess, the hospital was inevitable.

Bess had agreed with the change of plans thankfully as Sara turned into the driveway toward the emergency area. "Good idea, girl. I'd never make it into Doc's office." She spoke with economy, her breath short and gasping as she dealt with the pain that had exploded in her abdomen.

The entrance was beneath a portico and Sara made short work of running in the door to locate help. A gurney was brought without delay and in moments Bess had been surrounded by a team of nurses and an emergency room doctor. A phone call from the desk had located Dr. Richmond. Within minutes he had arrived, and without hesitation had diagnosed the problem.

The three hours she spent alone in the waiting room had seemed a lifetime to Sara. Bess had become much more to her than a housekeeper. Without words they had accepted each other. Without setting down guidelines, they had fit into a comfortable routine that suited them both. For Sara, Bess had become a friend, a much needed ally in the male household. Raised with men around her, she was used to their more abrupt, taciturn ways. Yet in her heart, she longed for female companionship. She sensed in Bess a warmth that had been missing in her girlfriends back home in Goose Creek. A more mature interest in her, a protective, unspoken aura of caring that enveloped her within its loose folds.

Now it would be her turn, she decided. She would

take care of Bess, watch over her when she was released from the hospital. Unknowingly, her shoulders lifted and then settled into a posture that spoke of strength and determination. She offered her hand to the doctor once more.

"Just tell me what I need to do, Dr. Richmond. I'm sure I can take care of Bess."

Clasping her slender fingers in his, he smiled. "I wouldn't be a bit surprised, Sara. She'll need to be off her feet most of the time until she's healed up. Regular meals after she gets home. No lifting, no straining, no heavy work for six weeks or so," he instructed.

"Cal will help me," Sara said. "Between us, we can make sure she doesn't overdo." Her face was resolute with determination. "I can do the cooking and housework."

For the first time in this long morning, Sam Richmond beheld loveliness. The rigors of emergency surgery had left only bloody memories of diseased tissue and torn flesh. His first impression of Sara had been of innocent beauty. But now, he caught a glimpse of her inner strength that lit her countenance as she announced her intentions. Her eyes glowed with purpose and her lips curved in anticipation. Sara was at her best during adversity and the challenge that faced her now took her whole concentration.

Cal lowered his brows as he looked down at her. "I can get you some help, Sara. You don't need to do it all."

Her hand waved away his offer. "I'll let you know if I can't handle it, Cal." She glanced at the nurses' desk and hesitated, her mind off in a different direction. "Will they let us know when we can see Bess?"

"She's going to be in recovery for a while. Why don't you go home and come back later? I'll tell her you'll see her this evening." Dr. Richmond edged toward the doorway, his thoughts already concentrated on morning rounds, and Sara and Cal nodded as he left them, then turned to face each other again.

"I'm sorry I wasn't here with you, Sara. I ran into some trouble and couldn't leave it. One of the men got snagged up in barbed wire when he tried to jerry rig a broken fence line. It took three of us to unwind him without cutting him up bad. Then we had to get the fence repaired before I was able to leave. I knew you were with Bess and Les Cochrane said you had things under control." He laid his arm across her shoulder as he turned her toward the elevator and they walked slowly in that direction.

"I was all right, Cal. Just worried and a little scared." She glanced up at him and he caught a trace of humor in her green eyes. "I think I broke all the speed limits getting here. Every time Bess moaned, I stomped down harder on the gas pedal." She felt the relief from tension as it bubbled up from the depths of her. "Do you think you can keep up with me on the way home?"

"I think I'd better take the wheel, Miss Leadfoot," he teased. "I had Les bring me in his car."

He dropped the weight of his arm to her waistline as the elevator door opened before them and they entered the small, empty cubicle. As the door slid shut, his other arm encircled her waist and she was once more pulled against his length. With a sigh, she leaned against him, greedy for the rare embrace he gave her. This was different from the sensual touching and holding of the night hours that nourished her feminine needs. This was a mutual sharing of affection that fed her womanly ego, that told her he gave, for this moment, his wholehearted approval of her.

He tipped her head back with a strong hand under her chin and his lips met hers in a kiss of affection and caring that offered relief from her fears. She felt the pent-up worry drain from her as she drew comfort from his nearness. They reluctantly broke apart as the elevator doors opened before them and they faced a lobby of people, waiting for the noon-time visiting hours to begin.

Sara's heart was light as they headed for home. Cal drove smoothly, his gaze falling on her frequently. She felt a freedom with him that was rare. And for now, she basked in his approval, her heart lifted by his nearness, her fragile ego fed by his words of appreciation.

"You came through like a champ, Sara," he said as he reached for her hand.

She felt the warmth of his fingers as they clasped hers and she clung to the acceptance he offered her with the gesture.

The presence of hungry men in the ranch house kitchen brought her back to earth with a thud. She flew into action and lunch became a fact in less than fifteen minutes.

To one man, she handed bowls and pointed to the silverware drawer. To another, she gave instructions for making coffee and to the third, she assigned the job of heating the soup and serving it. She sliced a loaf of the bread Bess had baked the day before and placed it on the table along with a bowl of sandwich spread from the refrigerator.

"Can you heat those baked beans in the microwave, Cal?" she asked as she dished up leftover potato salad.

"Yes, ma'am, I sure can," he answered with a grin, his eyes teasing and warm on her.

With the food assembled, the men sat to eat, hungry from their morning's work. They teased Ben about his dabs of pink antiseptic and his encounter with the barbed wire. Sara leaned against the counter and watched them, still driven by the events of the morning.

Her gaze focused on Cal and as if sensing her attention, he looked up, ignoring the men who bantered among themselves. His eyes were warm against her, moving over her face, then traveled slowly down, tracing a path that covered each curving line of her body.

She straightened, uncomfortable with his perusal, sensing the tingling arousal that was triggered by his nearness, his awareness of her. She flushed and he smiled, the corners of his mouth lifting only slightly as he looked once more at her face, noting the patches of color that told him she was aware of his thoughts.

Abruptly, she turned to the stove, seeking to move away from his appraisal. Lifting mugs from the cupboard shelf, she poured the coffee that had finished perking and placed a cup before each man at the table. Cal was last and she felt his warm hand against her back as he leaned out of her way. Her eyes flew to his and he nodded to the hallway beyond the kitchen, in a silent signal that she recognized.

After lifting four slices of apple pie from the glass plate on the countertop, she transferred the dessert to the table and slipped quietly from the room. Low voices followed her as she crossed the hallway to the living room and then faded as Cal followed her in and closed the double doors behind him.

He stood just inside the door and watched her as she turned in the center of the floor to face him. The room was a comfortable haven, created from the masculine assortment of furniture and accessories that had accumulated before her arrival in his life. She had added touches, small changes that had taken place so slowly, so subtly that he was hardly aware of them . . . until moments like this, when he saw her in the setting that she had formed. He watched her for a moment and the guilt that had become a part of him since their wedding night became a burden he could no longer bear.

"I haven't treated you right, Sara." His words were a surprise. She anticipated hearing orders from him concerning the house, perhaps his plans to visit the hospital, certainly not an apology.

"I'm not complaining, Cal," she said.

"You never have, and I guess that's what makes it even worse." He ran his fingers distractedly through his hair. "We got off on the wrong foot." He shook his head in denial and confessed, "No, that's not true. I'm the one who messed things up." He winced at the hopeful light in her eyes and words failed him.

How could he tell her of the battle that he fought daily? How could he speak of his unwarranted need for perfection in a wife? How could he deny her need for his wholehearted approval? He had been attracted to an image—a lovely girl who personified innocence, who had beguiled him with her green-eyed glances, who had twisted him into a hot, hurting bundle of need. And then, he had tracked her down and overwhelmed her with his vows and promises and brought her to his home, expecting her to be the very personification of his dream. Until he had realized that, although she was young and almost inexperienced, she nevertheless was not the innocent he had imagined.

"Hell! I didn't mean to cause you any pain, Sara. I was wrong to say anything to you." Without making a time reference, she knew exactly what he was speaking about. His words were burned in her memory and she blushed as she lowered her eyes, unable to face him in the bright afternoon sunlight that slanted in the windows.

"I should have told you, Cal."

He cut her off with a gesture. "I don't want you to say anymore about it, Sara. We'll forget it. And this time I mean it." Two longs steps brought him up against her and she leaned into his nearness, lifting her face, willing her eyes to meet his.

The shadow of pain that reached out to him from their depths stung his conscience and he sought to ease his guilt with her touch. His hands lifted hers and he touched her fingertips with his mouth. His lips opened and he whispered against her skin. "Thank you for today, Sara. I know I'm asking a lot of you, but I want you to know that I appreciate what you do here."

She started in surprise. "I didn't know that you even noticed me much around the house, Cal."

He looked up and his head shook slowly as he silently denied her accusation. "I'm aware of you all the time, little green eyes. I'm aware of what you have done to my house, to this room, to our bedroom. You've made a home out of this place. All your little knick-knacks and ruffles and pillows and such." He smiled ruefully. "I brought you here looking for the wrong things in a wife. I found out today that you have everything I need in a woman. You were here for me when you were needed."

He looked intently into her eyes. "I don't know what would have happened if you hadn't been here," he said. "You took care of Bess and you've taken hold here, in the house. I don't want you to do too much. I hope this isn't more than these hands can cope with."

His grip on her tightened and then he slipped her hands up to his shoulders and his own arms went around her in an embrace that began as an affirmation of his praise. His head lowered to hers and their lips met in a tender kiss that fed her need, and in that nourishment he found a whisper of desire that escalated like wildfire into burning flames that enveloped them.

The tension that had carried her through the morning exploded in his arms and she moved against him, seeking relief from the energy that surged within her.

His hands, no longer content to lie against her waist, traveled the length of her back, coaxing and then demanding her lithe body to form against his hardness, until she felt the beating of his heart as it matched her own pulse. Her fists gripped the curls that sprang into being as she ran her fingers through the thickness of his hair. She smoothed the ridges he had caused earlier with his own impatient hands and then relished the thrill of touching him with abandon, holding back none of the love she had hesitated to endow him with. Her eyes were closed and her mouth was alive beneath his, willing him to give and take the pleasure of his caressing lips.

He kissed her as if the wanting was uncontrollable within him. From whispering touches to unbridled hunger, he moved within seconds. Her response fired his need and his own awakened desire rose swiftly and surely as his seeking lips and tongue found the heated secrets of her mouth. His body was rigid and heavy with arousal and he spread his legs to hold her closer as he fed the passion that surged in his veins.

Forgotten were the men in the kitchen, neglected were the worrying thoughts of Bess that had plagued his morning. The only reality was in this room, in the body of this woman who gave so freely, who returned his burning, unspoken question with a need that brought her to immediate arousal.

He heard her quickened breathing; he felt the heat of her skin through the cotton shirt she wore. And he knew the restless movement of her hands as they left his head and face and traced the muscles of his shoulders and back, moving to his chest where probing fingers crept between the buttons of his shirt to find the curling patch of hair on his chest.

He left her for a moment and she swayed as if she would fall without his support, her eyes flying open in silent protest. But he had only retreated to the door, where he latched the lock that would insure them privacy. Then, with hands that trembled, he reached for her again and with arms that shook with his passion, he lowered her to the carpet, drawing her eager body against him as he whispered words of longing in her ear.

"Please, Sara. I need you. I need you right now, right here. Sara?" Her name was a plea and she answered it in the only way she knew how, with a soft, keening cry that told him of her own desire as she pulled at the buttons of his shirt, as she tugged it loose from the waistband of his jeans. And then she accepted his hands as they stripped the clothing from her and quickly removed his boots and jeans before he lowered himself once more to her warmth.

The loving was hard and fast. It was like nothing she had ever known and like nothing she had ever imagined. It was as if all of their newfound closeness in the midst of the tumult of the day's events had culminated in these few stolen moments. For he filled her with more than his aroused flesh, more than the physical touch of his body. Their need was for more than simple physical release and the shuddering spasms that held them in a close embrace vibrated with fierce intensity through her as she met his driving force with a strength she had not known she possessed.

He was her man—primitive knowledge that somehow had been brought to the forefront of her conscious mind. He belonged to her. For the first time in their marriage, she felt the closeness she had yearned for. He was hers, for this moment. In this hurried encounter that had caught them up in its intensity, he became a part of her.

Even the gradual withdrawal of his body could not take from her the fulfillment she had received. He touched her closed eyes with soft kisses and his voice was low and questioning. "Sara. Are you all right? Did I hurt you?" He felt a pang of deep regret as he remembered the force of his taking. Her slender body was still beneath him, only a shudder of breathing stirring her as she blinked and then focused on his face. She glowed with quiet joy and he sensed a contentment about her that was in direct contrast to the wild, clinging creature she had become only minutes before. He had not known she was capable of such passion and he felt a masculine pride in his ability to arouse her and satisfy her so thoroughly. His only regret was that he had been rough and hurried, that he had not wooed her and prepared her for his taking. But the woman who smiled at him appeared to have no such regrets.

"I'm fine, Cal. You didn't hurt me." She winced as she shifted beneath him. "This carpet leaves a little to be desired, though. I think I prefer our bed." She moved gingerly as he raised from her and then their hands met as he lifted her to her feet. Her fingers touched her flushed cheeks and she laughed softly.

"What must your men think of us?"

"Do you care?" He bent to her and touched a finger to the soft rise of her breast, smoothing away the reddened area that bore the marks of his whiskers. Almost absently he looked at her body, his eyes noting the lack of extra pounds that had disappeared during the summer. "You've lost weight, Sara." His hands touched her carefully, tenderly, as if he would make up for his hurried loving of her.

"I needed to get rid of a few pounds, Cal." She backed away, reaching for her clothing that was scattered across the couch and on the floor in front of it.

"You were fine, Sara. If you've been trying to lose weight, don't lose any more, will you?" He frowned down at her, more aware now of the slight lines of her frame. How had he not noticed before? With a groan of shame, he pulled her to him, her blouse and underwear crushed between them. "I'm sorry, Sara. For so much."

Her head lay against his chest and she heard the deep, heavy beat of his heart against her ear. She breathed a silent prayer of thanks for his words. She felt a moment's guilt as she recognized that without Bess's sudden illness, none of this would have come to pass today. And then she unashamedly relished the happiness that so unexpectedly filled her heart.

_____ SEVEN _____

The sun was hot, beating down on her back. Hotter
than yesterday, Sara thought as she sat back on her
heels. She reached into her pocket and found a bandana
of Cal's that she had borrowed from his drawer, wiping
it across her forehead to mop up the perspiration that
threatened to blind her momentarily. She eyed the pile
of carrots that lay next to her and decided that if she
didn't have enough for dinner, they could just have
seconds on salad.

That decision made, she pulled her basket closer. It
held a few tomatoes and green peppers and she pushed
them to one side as she made room for the rest of the
vegetables. It was too late to cook the squash, but if
she hurried she could clean and get the carrots ready
for the oven and stick them in with the roast.

A tired smile flitted across her face as she thought
of the huge roast that was cooking in the oven. She
had wanted to please Bess, perhaps tempt her appetite.
But this had to be one of the hottest days of the long
summer. Not one of my better decisions, Sara reflected.
She leaned back and wiped again at the sweat that

dripped from her forehead and looked up at the sky. Summer was determined to go out with a bang, keeping a tenuous grasp on the parched land. Rain was in the air and the clouds hung heavy in the west, but the breeze had died to a mere whisper as the afternoon drew to a close. It'll probably go around us, she thought, ruefully aware that never before had the weather been so important to her.

Cal had told her last night that if it didn't rain soon, the watering system, fed by deep wells, would be in trouble. It was the last thing she remembered him saying before she dozed off and only vaguely recalled his lips vainly coaxing her to respond as she hovered on the edge of sleep.

"I'm just plain tired!" Aware that she sounded like a cranky three year old, she looked around quickly and her laughter rang out as she mocked herself. I need to go in and get cooled off a little, she thought.

Getting up on her feet wasn't the problem, picking up the basket was. Her fingers were a mass of shallow cuts and gouges from slicing peaches and peeling tomatoes. The small nicks healed quickly, but working in the garden had lodged sand and dirt into each crack and crevice, and they were sore. But the jars on the shelf in the pantry and the rows of square containers in the freezer gave her a feeling of accomplishment she had rarely experienced before.

The man who watched her was torn between conflicting emotions. On one hand, he admired the spunky wife of Cal Hyatt and allowed his eyes to feast for a forbidden moment on her lithe body, so neatly covered and so unknowingly outlined by the sweat-dampened shorts and T-shirt she wore. On the other hand, he knew frustration as he noted the weary stance of the girl who stood, with head bowed, gathering her physical resources for another bout with the ranch house and its chores. He moved quickly.

"Let me take that." A large, brown hand reached to grasp the basket she held and Sara started in surprise.

"You startled me, Mr. Cochrane." Their neighbor stood just inside the gate of the kitchen garden and easily swung the load of vegetables from Sara's hands.

A slow smile lit his rugged features as he examined her. "Sorry, Mrs. Hyatt. Sure didn't mean to." She was suddenly aware of the damp knit fabric that clung to her body and the perspiration and dirt that were a result of kneeling in the garden in the hot sun. She wiped her hands on the seat of her shorts and winced as she scraped over a sore spot.

Les Cochrane was silent as he held the gate open for her and with a gallant gesture closed it behind them as she walked uncertainly toward the back porch.

"I just stopped by for a minute to see how Bess was coming along. Heard she got home from the hospital last week," he said.

Sara smiled, glancing back at him over her shoulder. "She'll be happy to see you, I'm sure. This has been a long day for her. Home from the hospital for two days and she thinks she's ready to be in the kitchen. She's been grumbling all afternoon about being laid up." A chuckle broke through as Sara thought about how ripe Bess's grumblings had gotten. "She threatened to find another job if I didn't let her out of bed a while ago."

"So, did you?" He reached past her and held the back screen door open as Sara moved past him, and then followed her to the sink. The basket of vegetables dangled from his right hand and she motioned for him to put it on the drainboard.

Sara dumped the carrots into the sink and ran water

to cover them as she reached for the brush. Something about Les Cochrane made her uncomfortable today. He leaned against the cabinet and watched her as she scrubbed at the carrots and then cut off the tops, and she felt the warmth of his eyes on her every move.

Her words were rapid, as if she felt the urge to fill the short silence that had fallen between them. "I let her get up. At least, I let her get as far as the couch in the living room. She was watching a game show when I went out to the garden a while ago." Her face was thoughtful as she turned to face their neighbor. "I've never thanked you properly for helping me the day she took sick. I was in a real bind, Mr. Cochrane . . ."

"Do you suppose you can call me Les?" His smile was admiring and his lean body was close. Sara stiffened. He caught her quick movement and backed up a step. "Sorry, ma'am, sure didn't mean to crowd you."

Sara took a deep breath, wishing futilely that Cal were at home and then met Les's look squarely.

"What does my husband call you, Mr. Cochrane?" As questions go, it was blunt, Sara thought, not sure if she was alienating a friend or insulting a neighbor.

"Well, mostly Les, I suppose. Unless he's upset with me, then he leaves off the mister and settles for Cochrane." He had retreated to the middle of the kitchen, his eyes still measuring the woman who stood before him. He nodded casually at the doorway to the hall. "Do you mind if I say hello to Bess?"

Sara turned from the sink, relieved at the distance he had put between them. "Let me see if she's awake first." She stepped softly through the door into the hall and then down a few steps to the living room. Bess was sitting on the couch, her feet on a low ottoman while the TV droned on unheard. Her head was tipped to one side and her eyes were closed, while faint soft snoring sounds blended with the laughter of the television audience. Sara backed up, easing the double doors closed behind her and returned quietly to the kitchen.

"I'm sorry, but she's dozed off and I'm sure you wouldn't want to wake her." Her words were apologetic as she approached Les Cochrane and he smiled in agreement.

"No, I wouldn't want to do that." He looked slowly around the big kitchen and then back at Sara. "There've been some changes in here. New curtains, aren't they?" He examined a picture Sara had hung over the kitchen table and then walked to the window where she had placed two planters of philodendron, one on either side.

The curtains were new, Sara had made them during her second week at the ranch from fabric she found in a trunk in the attic. Bess had sent her there to search for tablecloths and among Cal's mother's things, she had found a storehouse of fabric, clothing, and linens that had long been unused. A sewing machine sat under a dustcover beneath the eaves and she had coaxed Bess into helping her bring it downstairs. The curtains Les was admiring were her first effort and she was pleased at his words.

"Yes, I made the curtains. Bess has been so busy that she didn't have time for sewing and I've had more time than I've known what to do with."

"Not lately, I'll bet." His words were a growl as he turned back to her. "Hasn't Cal gotten you any help?"

"I haven't asked for any . . . I don't want any." She heard the sharp note in her voice and saw the surprise in Les's face. Then he grinned at her, at the saucy uptilted chin, at the curls that had escaped her ponytail and the independence that glared at him from her green eyes.

"You wouldn't have to ask if you were *my* wife."

His eyes approved her quietly, not encroaching on her but telling her of his admiration.

"She's not your wife, Cochrane." The voice was deep and harsh and Sara drew a deep breath as Cal appeared against the screen door.

Les's growl was lazy and teasing as he turned to face the cold glare of the man who had challenged him. "A fact I'm all too aware of, Cal." He lounged easily against the wall and ignored the anger Cal was struggling with. "I met your wife for just a moment the day Bess took sick and thought I'd get a chance to make it official today. Stopped by to say hello to Bess and found Sara digging in the garden. She looked about worn out to me." He straightened and glanced at his watch. "I think I'd better head for home. I brought Bess a bouquet of flowers from town. Have you got a jar or something to put them in, Sara?"

"Certainly, I'll find something." Sara glanced at Cal anxiously and at his nod opened the pantry door, reaching for the top shelf where she had seen several jars and vases.

"I'll just get them from the truck out front," Les said as he stepped into the hallway that led past the living room to the front door, Cal hard on his heels.

"Stay here, Sara," he threw the command over his shoulder and she obediently waited at the sink, rinsing the vase and wiping it dry slowly, listening all the time to the harsh murmur of voices that carried to where she stood. The truck door slammed and she heard the engine start before Cal came back into the room, a large bouquet of assorted blossoms in his hand. He thrust them at her angrily and then stood, fists propped against his hips as he watched her arrange them.

"How long has he been here, Sara?" She heard the

anger he no longer tried to supress and felt a tendril of unease whisper through her.

"Not long, Cal. I had just been picking vegetables for dinner and he carried the basket in for me. I was cleaning the carrots and then he asked to see Bess. And when I told him she was asleep, he stayed to talk for a minute." Her explanation was delivered in a voice that trembled and Cal was quick to respond.

He turned her to face him and set the vase down on the table with a thump that spilled a considerable amount of the water it held. "What else did he have to say, Sara? Besides telling you how soft you'd have it if you were his wife." She jerked back, eyes sparkling with anger that demanded release.

"You have no right . . . he didn't . . . I didn't." She shook her head in frustration and the soft flush that rose high on her cheekbones lent new beauty to her face. It was not lost on Cal and he was stunned with the waves of pure jealousy that swept over him.

"I have every right." The words were slow and measured, hard and furious and he spoke them in a dangerously soft voice that chilled Sara with its intensity. "You are my wife, Sara. I won't stand for you entertaining another man in my house. Especially a man who would so obviously like to have you for breakfast."

The flush faded from her cheeks and she felt a chill from within freeze her into a stiff, unbending creature as she leaned against the kitchen counter. "You're insulting me, Cal. I was being friendly to your neighbor. I am not responsible for his remark. In fact, I didn't like it any more than you did."

"If you have any complaints about overwork, you only have to say so, Sara. I offered to get you help and you turned me down flat. I came back to the house early this afternoon to give you a hand with supper and found you flirting with a neighbor. What was I supposed to think?" His tone had softened to a low snarl, accusing and harsh.

Tears trembled, ready to fall, and Sara turned away, stumbling as she tried to escape. Quick arms reached for her and she felt bruising hands catch her, setting her with little ceremony on a kitchen chair. She bowed her head and slapped at Cal's hand as he tried to turn her head to face him.

"Leave me alone, Cal . . . don't touch me." She took two deep breaths, willing the telltale tears to dry before they gave her away, even while she felt them spill over and trickle down her cheeks. "You'll have to think what you want to. The truth is, I didn't complain to Mr. Cochrane about being overworked. I was neighborly and friendly." She looked up at him and her green eyes glistened with tears and frustration. "I don't flirt, Cal. I don't complain and I don't flirt!"

"Don't you? Maybe not." He knelt by the chair and drew her to face him. "Sara, don't ever let me see his hands on you." At her indrawn breath and sound of protest, he shook his head. "Listen to me! Les Cochrane is a fine man and even though we've had our problems, he's a decent neighbor. But he's a lonesome man, a widower, alone with two little boys. As good a man as he is, I don't want him around my wife. Do you understand what I'm saying?"

"Yes." Her voice was dull and bleak, the anger gone, Cal's statement ringing loud and clear in her mind . . . "He's a decent neighbor . . . I don't want him around my wife."

"I understand, Cal." The pain was deep. It pounded at her in waves . . . he thinks I'm a tramp! He makes me feel so . . . so cheap! She pushed his hands away from her and slid from the chair, feeling the distance between them as never before. If he really thinks I'm interested in Les Cochrane . . . he doesn't even know me! The idea of playing temptress to another man had never occurred to Sara, but obviously that was the category Cal had placed her in.

"I need to finish dinner, let me be." She lifted the cleaned carrots from the sink and laid them to drain while she pulled the roasting pan from the oven. The heat escaped in a searing cloud and she felt perspiration break out on her brow before she could close the oven door. Cal's presence behind her was almost more than she could stand. Her hands shook as she lifted the cover from the pan and then arranged the carrots around the meat. She added a cup of water and replaced the lid.

"I'll do that." He left her no choice as he opened the oven door and slid the roasting pan inside. She offered no argument, but turned aside and began washing the basket of vegetables she had picked from the garden. Cal stepped closer.

"I said I'd help you. Why not let me finish those." She silently moved away from him and he watched her, seeing her as Les had, and found he could almost sympathize with the other man. No wonder he had looked at Sara with obvious admiration. She was lovely. Even in damp, clinging clothing, soiled from the garden . . . especially in the damp clinging shorts, he decided.

She had pulled her hair back early in the morning, catching it up in a ponytail that fell in a waterfall of long curls down her back. A profusion of shorter curls that had escaped, during the day clung now to her face and neck in a casual fashion that drew his eyes to her profile. The clean lines of her nose and forehead, the stubborn little chin that should have warned him of her Irish temper, and the set, folded lips that spoke silently of her withdrawal from him all served to make him more aware than ever of her beauty. In the T-shirt that boasted of containing "The World's Best Sister," she was the most appealing woman he had ever seen. Les Cochrane might well admire her; she was worth any man's admiration. But first and foremost, she was Cal Hyatt's wife.

His chin set in a determined line and even as she backed from the sink to give him access to the salad greens, he glared down at her with a possessive look— a look that was frightening in its power. The table was set in silence, the potatoes were heated in the microwave while Cal filled water glasses, and the roast was slid onto a platter while the hired hands washed on the back porch. Whether they felt the tension in the kitchen or not, they joked among themselves and complimented Sara on the meal.

She fixed a plate for Bess and carried it in on a tray, rousing the grumpy invalid with cheerful words.

"I've fixed your favorite dinner, Bess. Roast beef, just the way you told me you like it. Are you ready to eat?" She brought a table closer to the sofa and helped Bess to shift her position, easing the muscles that had become cramped while she slept.

"You slept through your game show," Sara teased gently as she eased down into an easy chair, stretching out her legs and watching Bess as she began to eat.

"Hmmph . . ." The sound was an acknowledgment of her teasing and Sara relaxed as she sank lower into the comfort of Cal's favorite chair. "Did I hear voices earlier?" Bess asked as she reached for her coffee cup. Her first spate of hunger satisfied, she sipped at the steaming brew.

Sara's brows lifted. "I was sure you were asleep, Bess. I checked on you . . ." She made an impatient gesture, her fingers spread as she smoothed back the wayward strands of hair from her face. "Les Cochrane stopped in to visit with you. In fact," she lifted herself with a show of effort from the chair, "he brought you flowers. I had forgotten them."

"Let it wait, missus." Bess waved her back and with a tired smile Sara dropped back, her sigh deep as she closed her eyes briefly. "You're working too hard," Bess scolded. Her keen eyes noted the roughened hands that were relaxed and upturned on Sara's lap. "You've managed to skin up about every finger you got, girl."

"I've never done canning and freezing before," Sara admitted. "Peeling potatoes for my family was about the extent of my carving ability." She inspected her hands with a critical eye. "It's just that my skin is dry. Maybe cream would help . . ." She slid forward in the chair and her grin was cocky as she bragged. "I've got over forty quarts of tomatoes canned, Bess, and I froze a bushel of peaches and over a bushel of green beans." She spread her fingers and inspected them closely with a frown and then another quick smile lit her face. "I don't mind not having pretty hands, Bess. I'm turning into a real ranch wife."

"You get you some gloves out of the shed when you work in the garden, missus." Bess's instructions left no room to argue.

"Yes, ma'am, whatever you say," was the meek reply and Bess grinned as Sara rose to take the tray from her.

"Let me help you." She moved the table and eased her weight behind Bess's efforts to rise from the couch, offering her hands and levering her to her feet.

"Another few days should get me back in business," Bess announced stoutly as they made the return trek down the hall to the large, airy bedroom at the back of the house. Sara smiled gently and declined to reply. She knew that the rigors of surgery and the attendant recovery period were taking their toll, and she vowed to keep the older woman from kitchen duty as long as possible. Her walking was almost back to normal, just getting up and down still presented a bit of a problem. But Sara was determined to coddle and pamper as much as Bess would allow.

"Did you eat yet?" The bed gave with her weight as Bess sat down and she eyed the slender figure before her. "You got to keep up your strength, girl. You'd better get in there and snatch a bite before those men eat it all."

Sara nodded and turned to the door. "I think they're all done. I'll clean up and relax with mine out on the porch." She hesitated and glanced back. "Call me if you need anything, hear?"

"Get going now. I don't need you hovering over me." The grumble was purely for effect and they both knew it, but Sara scooted out the door hastily and then sobered as she reached the kitchen.

Cal stood at the sink, rinsing plates and stacking them next to the cups and silverware on the drainboard. He looked up with a glance that took in her hesitant pose just inside the doorway. "I'll leave these for you to put in the dishwasher, Sara. The food is still on the table. Make sure you eat something." He was abrupt as he wiped his hands on the towel and turned away, and her eyes filled with tears.

Things had seemed better between them, especially since Bess's surgery. His jealousy today, if that's what it truly was, had been unfounded, from Sara's point of view. But obviously, from Cal's angle, she was on the make. She smiled sadly. She'd never been on the make for anyone. But, she argued with herself, if Cal was jealous, maybe it proved that he cared about her. Or else he just considered her to be his private property . . . like the ranch and his horses. The thought was not comforting, she decided.

The love she felt for him was so overpowering at times that it was all she could do to contain it. She ached to tell him of her feelings, but held the words back, instinctively protective of her love, afraid to face his rejection. His ability to cause her pain was tremendous. She saw no reason to give him any more power than he already wielded over her. She mulled over the unfairness of his accusations this afternoon. Les had been a little forward, but she had felt able to handle it. His eyes on her had been admiring, but not insulting, and his jibes at Cal had been made in an offhand manner. She thought of the man who lived next door. He took care of two sons with no help in the house. He ran a small spread with just one hired hand and he tended his own business. No, Cal had no right to accuse . . . she shook her head. Cal didn't abide by the rules, he made his own.

She picked up the plate she had prepared and put it in the microwave, then waited for it to heat. The sun was heading for the horizon, the porch at the back of the house would be cool. The porch swing would soothe her wounded feelings and ease her tired body.

She heard the phone ring just as she eased her way out of the screen door and hastily backed up, leaving her dinner on the table as she went to answer.

"Sara!" Only Marcie could start a conversation that way and Sara's heart lifted at the sound of Marcie's voice.

"Hi, stranger." She felt the tension ease from her body as she closed her eyes, pleased by the sound of Marcie's familiar greeting.

"Sara, I'd like to come visit. Is it too soon after the wedding? Do you have room for me? Can you send me directions?" The questions flew fast and furious and Sara's smile widened with each one.

"No, yes, yes!" She laughed aloud and the sound was welcome to the ears of the man who stood outside the house. Cal hesitated on the porch steps, waiting for Sara to finish on the telephone before he interrupted her. His conscience was bothering him and he had halfway decided to apologize to her for his behavior, heading back to the house before he reached the barn. The sound of the phone ringing had halted him and the rare laughter of his wife increased his discomfort.

"She hasn't had much to laugh about lately, Hyatt," he grunted under his breath as he turned and sat on the steps. His anger had been directed at Les Cochrane but he had taken it out on her and, with a sigh, he admitted to himself that he was being unfair. If Sara had had a dozen lovers before their marriage, it was in the past. Even as he thought it, he knew the figure was grossly exaggerated and he shook his head. But he still didn't want Cochrane alone with Sara. She was too tempting and Les was ripe for a woman. If he took advantage of a situation, it would cause problems that would damage relations between the two men permanently.

The screen door opened behind him and he heard her breath catch as she spotted him. "Cal! I thought you had gone out back." She came out the door, a plate balanced in one hand, her glass of iced tea in the other.

He stood quickly. "Here, let me help you." He caught the door and she smiled, pleased at the change in his demeanor. The porch swing still beckoned, but she turned away from it and sat down on the step, next to where he had been perched.

"Come sit with me, Cal. That was Marcie on the

phone. She's coming down for a visit. She'll be driving down in a few days.'' Her excitement was almost alive in the glow of her skin, in the sparkle that lit her eyes, and in the dimples that came and went in her cheeks. "It's all right, isn't it?" She was apprehensive as he frowned at her.

He swallowed the quick reluctance that almost spurred him to speak and then simply nodded. Sara, so wrapped up in her news, smiled at his halfhearted approval and talked on. She ate, chewing and swallowing, hardly noticing what she did, until the plate of food was gone. She looked up in surprise.

"I didn't know I was so hungry. I really made short work of that, didn't I?" She sighed and set the plate aside, then leaned back on her outstretched arms, her slender profile outlined against the setting sun. "I'll put her to work, Cal." Her smile was mischevious. "Can you imagine Marcie cooking for four men?" Her expressive look was speculative. "Come to think of it, she just may enjoy it. Men are Marcie's favorite thing." Her mind switched midstream. "I'll have to fix up one of the spare bedrooms. Maybe I'll have time to make new curtains . . ."

"Whoa, slow down, Sara. Marcie will be fine without any fussing on your part. She's not coming here to check out our guest rooms, she's coming to see you." His drawl was teasing and she felt a lightening of her spirit. Cal was trying to make amends. She could feel it in his mood and even though their problems still existed, she could not reject his olive branch.

"You really don't mind, do you, Cal. If she comes, I mean?" He caught the anxious tone under her words and he shook his head slowly.

"No, I don't mind, Sara." The doubt still nudged at him. Marcie was up to something, he couldn't imagine what she found attractive about visiting Sara on a ranch. She had been noncommital about their marriage, sending a congratulatory card and a short note, but Cal had sensed her attitude. Marcie thought Goose Creek was too far out of the mainstream of life. A weathered cattle ranch in the middle of Florida surely was not her idea of Vacationland, U.S.A. He decided wisely to reserve his opinion and instead leaned against the post and tugged Sara over until she lay against him.

"Do you suppose you can stay awake for a while? I have to finish up out in the barn and then I'll be in." His words were warmly suggestive in her ear and she leaned into his solid chest, her head turning until she could touch his throat with her lips.

The whisper was warm against him. "I'll be awake, I promise." His arms tightened briefly and then he put her aside and she watched as he strode away from her, her eyes filled with the love that she could not speak.

EIGHT

The rusty blue pinto had seen better days, but the woman who drove it was beyond caring about appearances. Marcie, too, had seen better days. She listened to the engine's wheeze for a few seconds before she turned off the ignition.

"I don't know how you did it, old girl." The smile that lifted her mouth from its grim lines paid tribute to the sturdy little car. She opened the door and slid from the seat, flexing her back as she leaned on the door frame.

Sara didn't know whether to smile or sympathize. Marcie was a bit the worse for wear, her clothing wrinkled, her makeup almost nonexistent, her complexion wan and pale. Sara decided to compromise.

"It's good to see you!" She grinned and then frowned as she held Marcie by the shoulders. "Rough trip, Marcie? You look a little wiped out."

"A little? Let's be honest, kiddo." Marcie was so relieved to be with Sara after two long days on the road; to be welcomed, literally, with open arms that she found herself hovering between tears and laughter. She looked down at her wrinkled clothing disdainfully.

"I'm a wreck. I slept in a rest area last night and had to choose between sweating in the heat or leaving the windows open and fighting off bugs. And then I woke up every few minutes, just keeping an eye out for wandering night drivers."

Sara turned to the house and her arm squeezed the other woman's waist for a moment. "Come on inside and get something cool to drink. The men can carry in your stuff when they come up for dinner."

They walked single file through the gate and Sara waved a hand at her garden, its last brave efforts waiting for harvest. Yellowed vines withered around the few squash and melons that still needed to be picked. The last of the tomatoes hung heavily on plants that sagged to the ground and a few green peppers were turning red.

Marcie cast a sideways glance at her friend. "This is how you spend your time?" She shuddered visibly. "You've turned into a farmer, Sara."

"Looks that way." Sara stuffed her hands into her pockets. "I'm a rancher's wife, Marcie." Her smile was smug as she considered her situation. "I used to buy the food and cook it for my dad and my brothers. Now, I grow part of it and freeze it and can it. I found I can sew a little . . ."

"Enough, enough!" Marcie slung an arm over Sara's shoulders and squeezed with affection. "I believe you! I should have known that an old-fashioned girl like you would fit right in here."

The screen door closed behind them as they stepped into the cooler air that was circulated through the kitchen by a window fan. The scent of dinner cooking moved Sara into immediate action and she turned quickly to the stove.

"Have a seat, Marcie, while I finish this up. Tell me

all your news.'' Her smile faded as she glanced over her shoulder. Marcie was slumped in a chair at the table and her eyes were bleak as she wiped at a line of perspiration that outlined her upper lip.

''Marcie?'' Sara's voice was hesitant as she knelt beside the chair. ''What is it? What's wrong?''

''She's pregnant, Cal.'' Her head was tucked into his shoulder and Cal felt the softness of her breath against his throat as Sara spoke. She tugged the quilt higher over them and her fingers drifted back to settle uneasily against his chest. He waited patiently and the silence was long between them.

''Cal?'' The thread of uncertainty was there and he took pity on her.

''I heard you, Sara.'' His sigh was deep as he turned, displacing her from the shelter of his arms. He leaned over her in the darkness, his skin a contrast against the white sheet that covered them. She lifted her hands and rested them on his shoulders, still uncertain of his mood.

''I didn't know before she came, Cal.'' The words were hasty, her tone apologetic as she tried to explain. ''She told me when she got here.'' Her eyes searched for some trace of his reaction, but the shadows hid him from her. Only the tension that radiated from his body gave her a clue and she plunged ahead.

''Cal, she wants to stay . . . for awhile. I told her I'd ask you.'' She felt his body shift and his head lifted as he looked away from her.

''Please, Cal . . .'' She was prepared to beg. Marcie had once been her best friend and Sara could not turn her back easily.

''You're a sucker for the lost sheep, aren't you, girl?'' His cynical tones were not lost on Sara and she let her hand fall from his arm. Her reflex action and the quick intake of breath told him that his remark had stung. He relented.

"I'm sure we can find room for her, Sara. Just don't let her cause a lot of extra work for you and Bess." He flopped over to his back and rested his head on one palm, the other hand reaching for hers, letting her know that he was not angry.

Their fingers touched and he gripped her hand. "Whose is it?"

"She didn't say . . . just that it wasn't important about the father. He gave her money for an abortion, Cal." The word was distasteful to her and she spoke it with fierce disgust. "She used the money to come here. She has a little saved up and she thinks she can find a job and work till the baby comes."

"Then what?" Cal turned back to her and caught her close to him. He pulled her against him and buried his face against her throat where the sweetness of her scent drew him.

Her voice was muffled against his hair. "I don't know what she'll do then." He felt her inhale as if to speak again and then she sighed, her breath warm against his temple.

A faint irritation pricked at his conscious mind. He wanted Sara all to himself, without distraction.

"Forget Marcie for tonight." The words were muttered into her throat as he surrendered to the subtle spell she wove so unknowingly about him. His hand slid down her back and he tugged at her gown, while his lips traced a path that began with the softness of her mouth. His hand gripped her hip and turned her, following with the easy slide of his body over hers as he crushed her into the mattress.

"Am I too heavy?" His whisper was muffled against

the bodice of her nightgown as his head dipped to the low neckline, his teeth worrying at the ribbon that tied it in front.

Her fingers enclosed his face for a moment as Sara lifted him from her, and he waited and watched silently as she untied the bow that was keeping him from the prize he searched for. His mouth was hot against her skin and she shuddered, her eyes closing helplessly as the now familiar tendrils of pleasure began to build.

"Cal . . ." She needed to be closer. She welcomed the weight of his body and strained to pull him even tighter to her, her arms over his shoulders, fingers tensing into the firm muscles of his back. His easy acceptance of Marcie's visit was welcome to Sara. His uneasy acceptance of Marcie's pregnancy had soothed her worry for a while. Now, his seeking hands threatened to put Marcie entirely out of her mind and she surrendered to the touch of hard, calloused fingers that brought hot, damp pleasure to her so easily.

Her shuddering breath and her involuntary movements brought him to the brink too quickly, and Cal found himself once more at the mercy of his need for her. He groaned as he lifted his upper body, bracing himself with his palms flat on either side of her shoulders. And then he moved slowly as she shifted to accommodate him, and her hands slipped between their bodies as she guided him until he found the hot, pulsing pleasure he sought in the heated flesh of her body.

The kitchen is apparently the center of this house, Marcie thought as she stood in the doorway. Twice a day the table was surrounded by all seven of them—the hands, Cal, Sara, Bess, and herself.

Lunch was the exception. The men ate quickly. Cal was usually in a hurry when they came back to the house in the middle of the day. Other days, Sara loaded food into the pickup truck and drove to where the men worked to deliver their noon meal.

Privately, Marcie wondered how Sara stood it. Catering to men had never been high on Marcie's list of priorities. She preferred being catered to, and only the sideways glances of the three hands and the frankly appraising looks she encountered on occasion kept her spirits up. She watched as the four men at the table finished their lunch and then left the kitchen.

Cal slid an arm about his wife as he passed the stove and her soft smile pleased him as he dropped a quick kiss on her forehead. The screen door slammed behind him and Marcie sauntered to the window.

"Does the kiss make it all worthwhile, Sara?" Her tone was only half-teasing and Sara hesitated. Marcie was so unpredictable. Her moods varied from slightly cynical to overly enthusiastic.

"I don't mind cooking for Cal and the men. Bess is almost back to her old self and we share the work," Sara said quietly.

Although the summer had been difficult at times, Sara was content. Cal was more open with her and with a smile of resignation, she admitted to herself that his approval and appreciation were all she needed to make her life satisfactory. The nagging need that pricked at her during the dark hours of the night was her thorn in the flesh, she had decided. Cal might never come to love her, but he wanted her and she knew he needed her.

She sensed that he fought sometimes against the flaring desire she was able to kindle in him so easily, but it was there and she derived satisfaction from it. Perhaps love was not an issue with men . . . Cal never mentioned the word.

A shadow that fell across the kitchen floor halted Sara's musings and she heard Marcie's quick intake of breath.

"We have company . . ." Marcie's fingers ran quickly through her blond hair and she turned to face Les as he stepped through the door. His eyes touched her and answering warmth drew him to approach her.

"Marcie." His nod was quick and his look was all encompassing as it swiftly ran down her body and back, and then focused on her face. She flushed, knowing he was aware of the slight mound of her pregnancy.

"Hi, Les." Her instincts were seldom wrong where men were involved and she felt again the sure knowledge that Cal's neighbor was unwillingly attracted to her. Four weeks at the ranch had brought her into contact with him several times, each time making her more aware of his scrutiny.

He turned from her and his nod at Sara was respectful. "Sara." The single word was given in greeting and Sara acknowledged it with a quick nod and a smile.

"The men have gone back out already, Les. Did you want to see Cal?"

He shook his head in answer. "Not really, Sara. I came to see Marcie." He motioned to a chair and Marcie caught a quick breath as she sat down at the table.

"Here I am, cowboy," she teased. "What can I do for you?"

Les pulled out another chair and with an inquiring look at Sara, he sat down gingerly, as if afraid the chair might not hold him. "I have a problem, Marcie. I'm hoping you can help me with it."

His big hands held the Stetson that he had removed upon entering the kitchen and he played with the rim, choosing his words carefully as he spoke. "My boys need a little supervision after school. You know—

homework assignments and chores and getting dinner going." He glanced up at her and found her watching him with a puzzled look.

"Are you asking me to babysit for you, Les?" Her tone was incredulous and he flushed, his fingers tightening on the hat he held.

"Not really, Marcie. I just thought you might be able to use some extra money. With me working outside and not able to keep an eye on things, the boys tend to get a little out of hand. They just need someone there to sort of supervise." He shifted in the chair and Marcie made a quick decision.

Jobs were not plentiful here, as four weeks of scouring the want ads had told her. Models were not in great demand in this section of Florida, and her condition would not have been conducive to working in the public eye for very long in any job. Fast-food establishments made up the major portion of prospective employers in town and Marcie could not face long hours on her feet at this stage. It had been easier to lay back and enjoy Sara's hospitality.

"I guess I could do that . . . but I'm not much of a cook. I can try it anyway, for awhile." Her tentative acceptance brought a broad grin to the tall rancher's face.

"Can you start today?" he asked. He was counting heavily on this idea to work. It would throw them together on a daily basis and Les was all in favor of anything that would put Marcie into his life. He had sensed an attraction for her that was not deterred by the fact of her pregnancy. The idea of having her watch the boys had been inspired, he decided.

It would be a gamble, Marcie thought. The man was good looking, a little older than anyone she had ever been interested in, but he sure was a solid citizen . . .

unlike some of the other men she had met in the past few years. He had been polite, but attentive during their previous encounters. Today, he was openly admiring and Marcie found herself responding to his warmth. Besides, he might be a way out of her problems, she reflected.

Sara watched the silent exchange of glances and turned away as she recognized the calculating look that Marcie quickly hid. She'll always land on her feet, she thought. But Marcie might be in for a surprise. Les was not the strong, dumb rancher she took him for. He was taking a risk, asking Marcie into his home, but Sara knew with surety that he knew what he was doing. Perhaps he saw something in Marcie that had eluded the men in New York. Maybe there was hope that he could strip aside the layers of pseudo sophistication that Marcie wore like a shield. Underneath her clever words and brittle demeanor was the girl from Goose Creek who had been Sara's best friend in the years of their youth. And that person was worthy of Les's attention, perhaps his affection.

"I could come over now, Les." Before she could change her mind, before the thought of coping with two young boys and the inherent problems that might follow, she decided to take the plunge.

Chafing at her dependency, she had been getting restless. And although Sara and Cal had made her feel welcome, she knew that another chance to earn her own way might not come along quickly. Her smile was warm but Sara caught the uneasy movement of Marcie's hands as she rose, her fingers finally coming to rest on the edge of the table.

"Let me get my keys, Les," she said, "and I'll follow you home." She turned to the hallway and climbed the stairs at his nod of acceptance.

Then he turned to Sara. "You haven't said anything, Sara. Do you mind that I've borrowed your houseguest?"

She sensed his unsureness. He had kept his distance from her for weeks, aware of the protective jealousy that Cal shrouded her with.

Sara leaned against the counter and hesitated. Her fingers folded the dish towel she held as she fluctuated between loyalty to her friend and honesty with her neighbor. Perhaps she could satisfy both impulses, she decided.

"I don't mind, Les. Marcie needs to be doing something productive. Maybe this will work out for both of you." Her eyes finally met his and he was aware of her struggle.

"I'm a big boy, Sara. I lived in Atlanta before we came to Florida and I've seen a lot of women like Marcie." A wry twist of his lips almost passed for a smile as he paused. He shrugged as he admitted, "She's not what I would have chosen to be attracted to." His big hands turned the hat in his hands as he spoke. "I don't even understand it myself, right now. I just know that I'd like to give it a chance, see if there isn't a little of the small-town girl left in her."

He lifted his shoulders in a helpless shrug. "I really do need someone for the boys, you know. They're good kids, but they get into scraps and their homework gets neglected. I think they'll like Marcie."

The new routine was pleasing to Sara. Marcie left each morning before breakfast and returned after dinner at night. She was slowly becoming accustomed to Les and his boys, and Sara was pleased at the gradual change in her friend's attitude. From careless, cynical remarks she had progressed to humorous, often affectionate descriptions of the adventures she had encountered while putting Les's house in order. Her accounts were full of the boys, but Les was surprisingly absent in the reports she gave daily. As if she were hoarding her thoughts of her employer and mulling over them in private, Sara thought.

Once more allowed to assume almost her full quota of household chores, Bess donned an apron and took back control of her kitchen.

Sara had to admit to herself that Marcie's absence was welcome. It was good to be back to normal, now that their guest had taken up partial residence next door.

"Do you think she can handle it?" Bess sounded doubtful even as she posed the question.

"I don't know why not," Sara answered. "I remember when we were kids, she used to babysit to earn money for makeup. She had a lot of jobs, so I guess she must have been good at it." Her smile was soft, remembering.

"When I was still reading Nancy Drew mysteries, Marcie was planning on being a model and practicing with all sorts of pots and bottles and brushes. She always had to wash it off before her mother came home from work, but I remember lying on her bed and watching her with a makeup mirror, making herself beautiful. She had such dreams . . ."

Her teeth touched her bottom lip and her eyes were sad as she remembered their closeness, aware that even then Marcie had chosen to take risks in order to seek her own idea of happiness. "When she was eighteen, she left Goose Creek with enough money to get to New York and rent a room to stay in." Sara shook her head slowly and grinned. "That was Marcie . . . sure that she could make it. And she might have, if the breaks had been right. As it was, she never hit the right combinations . . . never made the right connections." Sara's sigh told the story . . . Marcie had missed the mark, made bad choices.

"Well, I hope she's not trying any of her shenanigans on Mr. Cochrane," Bess sniffed. "He's a good man and if he thinks she's mother material for those boys of his, he's got another think coming." Unlike Cal, she had made no secret of her opinion of Sara's friend. Even though Les seemed to be satisfied with Marcie's performance as combination sitter and cook, Bess doubted the competence of the young woman. She and Marcie had not hit it off well.

Their voices rose and fell, and in the living room Cal listened, catching the drift of their conversation. He had tried, for Sara's sake, to be obliging and courteous; his only irritation being Marcie's tendency to let Sara wait on her. He derived a secret delight from Bess's dark looks as she watched her young "missy" being put upon, and he wondered if Sara was even aware of what a champion she had in their housekeeper.

"Don't worry about Les Cochrane." Cal joined them, standing in the doorway, one arm leaning against the frame, the other hand stuck in his back pocket as he watched his wife finish tidying the kitchen. Sara glanced up, unaware that he had been listening to the conversation.

"I'm not worrying, Cal. Bess is just stewing a bit." Her eyes were lacking their usual sparkle, he thought. She had been tired lately and he hadn't done much to brighten her life. She had had it much easier in South Carolina, with her family looking after her, with her job and friends to occupy her time. Her slender shoulders slumped a little as she turned to him and he thought of all the hours she spent in this kitchen everyday. His hand slid out of his pocket and he reached for her, enclosing her waist with his arm as he turned her toward the back door.

"Forget Marcie for now, Sara. Let's go sit on the swing for a while." The surprise on her face faded to a pleased smile as they settled in the padded-wooden seat. He set the swing in motion with one foot and she leaned against his chest, determined to enjoy this unexpected break from their usual routine. His hand on her was warm and soothing as he moved his fingers against her skin. With lazy motions, he caressed her arm and she reached to capture his hand. Her eyes closed and she drew his fingers close to her face, brushing her cheek against the callouses that never softened.

"You work too hard, Cal." She stifled a yawn as she spoke and he chuckled, the sound muffled against her hair.

"I was just thinking the same thing about you, Mrs. Hyatt." A breeze blew softly through the vines that still clung to the trellis on the end of the porch. The sun was going down and the temperature had begun to fall a little. She snuggled closer and her sigh of contentment touched him.

"Sara?"

"Hmmm?" She turned his hand against her face and her lips found a soft spot in the center of his palm. The innocent gesture was his undoing.

She could dispel his doubts, creep past his walls. So unknowingly, she touched him and he was filled with an emotion that defied his logic. Admitting that he wanted her was easy. The need he felt for her body was always hovering just beneath the surface and he found himself resenting it sometimes. He wondered briefly and bitterly what other man had experienced the same need. What other hands had touched her. Helplessly, his thoughts tangled, jealousy of an unknown part of her past twisted through him. His hands turned her in his arms and he crushed her lips beneath his in a kiss that spoke of anger.

Her response was startled and she jerked against him, shaken from the reverie that had enveloped her. She recognized the anger. It had been a part of their love-making before and she relaxed beneath his touch. Her mouth felt bruised beneath his, but she opened her lips and gave him the opening he was seeking. Her body shifted a bit, softening against him, easing her arm up until her fingers were buried in his hair, until she felt his anger subside into desire and she knew that he had overcome it once more.

His hands gentled, his mouth softened, and he soothed her lips with touches that apologized for his roughness. "Sara . . ."

Her fingers eased between their lips and she pressed them gently against his mouth. "Hush, Cal. It's all right." She understood the anger, she knew its source. Until he could accept her as she was, it would come between them.

He took her fingers inside his mouth and bit lightly at them, deliberately breaking the mood he had created. "I think I hear a car coming. Probably Marcie."

He lifted her from him and deposited her back in the corner of the swing. "She'll want to talk to you." His hand brushed against her cheek and she felt the unspoken apology in his touch. He would be gentle and tender tonight . . . his eyes held the promise and she accepted it gladly.

NINE

"Who'd ever have thought that I'd be spending my days with my nose in a cookbook?" Marcie's tone was incredulous as she bent over the kitchen table searching through the index for a recipe.

Sara paused on her way to the pantry, her arms clutching two bags of groceries. "If you come up with some wonderful ideas for using leftover roast beef, let me know," she said pleadingly.

She pushed through the swinging doors and caught them deftly with her shoulder. The countertop on one side held her burden and she quickly emptied the bags, distributing them to the pantry shelves that held the food supply for her household. She surveyed them with satisfaction. The top of the pantry held the summer's bounty that had lent itself to canning, and her lips pursed in an assessing smile as she noted the jars of pickles and preserves lined up neatly. Secretly, she hugged to herself the sense of pleasure that this part of her life had given her.

"I wonder if I'm a throwback to pioneer days?" Her voice carried to the kitchen and Marcie lifted her head, her finger holding the spot she had finally decided held the answer to her menu problem.

"You probably would have been right at home as a homesteader, Sara." She blew idly at a lock of hair that had escaped her loosely held together top-knot. The casual look was definitely "in" on a ranch, she had decided as she looked in her mirror this morning. Spiked hair and manicured nails were things of the past. The switch to a more casual appearance was part of her decision to adapt. And now, looking the part she was committed to playing, to her surprise, came easily. Her admiration and gratitude where Sara was concerned was grudging at times, but more and more it seemed that Sara had chosen well. And each day that passed made her more aware that she had chosen wisely in seeking her friend's help.

Marcie considered Sara as she pushed through the swinging doors into the kitchen. She frowned at her with a measuring look and was only half jesting as she spoke. "You know, I can almost see you . . . driving a covered wagon . . ."

"Not quite," Sara countered. "I'm too spoiled by electricity and flush toilets and Cal's big freezer out back. Although I might have done all right . . ." She hesitated and her smile softened. "I think I was cut out for this kind of life, Marcie. All the years growing up, after my mother died when I had to do for my dad and the boys, I never really minded. Even when I worked in Mr. Carson's law office, I enjoyed the work at home more than I did the typing and filing and all."

She sat down at the table and propped up her elbows, leaning her chin on her folded fingers. "Living here has been easier for me than anyone realizes. My dad thinks I work too hard, Cal tries to make me slow down, and Bess thinks I do too much of her work.

None of them realize that I do it because it suits me. I like making a home for Cal, fixing things up and learning to please him.''

Marcie shook her head. Her opinion of Cal's taciturn moods was better unspoken, she decided. ''You do too much, you know. In fact, you've always tried to do it all. Cal and your dad and Bess are right.''

She shifted in her chair and straightened uneasily. Her hand rested for a moment on the mound that was daily becoming more apparent below her waist. ''When I've had this baby, after my life gets straightened out again, I'm going to find someone who will try to please me and give me what I need.'' She gestured widely at the kitchen. ''This is okay if it suits you, but I need more.''

A sadness that tore at her brought quick tears to her eyes and Marcie blinked them back. Her chin lifted and she tightened her lips, denying the quiver that would give her away. ''We're totally different people . . . I could never figure out how we managed to be friends.''

Sara's eyes were wise and, not for the first time, she caught a glimpse of the tendencies Marcie tried so hard to subdue. She saw beyond the cynical, casual attitudes that protected Marcie's more vulnerable side. She saw the need for love and approval that Marcie covered with flip remarks and sophisticated jokes. Sara chose carefully who she would give her love to and Marcie had long since been one of those whom she cared about.

''We're friends because we've always needed each other,'' she said finally. She touched Marcie's slender fingers that had so recently become accustomed to housework. The nails were filed shorter and polish was noticeably absent, but the beauty of Marcie's hands was not dimmed by the work they had been doing.

"I used to envy you when we were in school, you know." Sara's quiet admission sent Marcie's eyebrows soaring.

"You're kidding!"

"No, really. You were so slim and tall and so sure of what you wanted to do. You always knew how to fix your hair and your hands were always beautiful." Sara compared her smaller, tanned fingers, nails clipped and short; then turned her hands over to show Marcie the calloused spots on her palms. Her fingers traced the small scars that were fading, her mementos of the gardening, canning, and freezing she had done. She grinned with amusement at the difference. "I'd never have made it as a hand model, would I?"

She clasped Marcie's fingers tighter. "I always knew you'd make it, though. I was so proud of you."

"But I didn't make it." The admission was hard to make, but Marcie demanded honesty of herself where Sara was concerned. "I made some money at it, but I never hit the big time. I never was able to make the right connections, meet the right people."

She leaned back in her chair and her hands pulled from Sara's as she touched again the evidence of her pregnancy, her fingers caressing in circular movements as her eyes softened momentarily. "If it hadn't been for this . . ." She looked down at herself and then up at Sara again. "If I hadn't gotten pregnant, I'd probably still be scrambling for jobs, still be struggling to pay the rent."

Her mouth lifted in a fleeting smile. "I'm almost glad it happened, you know." She looked surprised as she realized the truth of her confession. "I really am! I was getting tired of the rat race and I think I knew that I'd never find what I needed in New York. I don't know if I'll find it here either, but maybe I stand a better chance.''

The time for confidences was over and, as if she had donned a mask, Marcie stood to her feet and her grin was cocky as she clutched the cookbook to her breast. ''I'll try not to poison the Cochrane's tonight. Maybe they'll go for my version of beef and noodles.'' She rolled her eyes in pretended horror. ''I am so sick of eating Les's cows. I'd give my eye teeth for a lobster!''

''You wouldn't know how to cook it if you had one.'' With a laugh, Sara bluntly punctured Marcie's complaint. And then her smile salved the wound. ''And it probably wouldn't agree with you, anyway. You're in cattle country, Marcie. Beef is in!''

''You're telling me!'' Cookbook in hand, she turned to leave and then her mood became pensive for a moment. ''Sara . . . you're right, you know. I do need you, I always have. You're the only friend I've been able to count on through the years.''

Before Sara could reply, even before she realized fully that Marcie had, for the first time, acknowledged the importance of their friendship to herself, the screen door had slammed shut and Marcie was gone—on her way to the blue Pinto that carried her daily to the Cochrane ranch.

Les Cochrane had problems. Two rambunctious boys and more work than he had time to deal with were at the top of his list.

Housekeepers had been his answer when the boys were younger, but they had been, for the most part, unreliable and he found it simpler to cope with the cooking and laundry himself during the evenings.

Offering Marcie a job had only served to create

another problem for him. One he had become aware of even before she entered his home for the first time.

He found her presence addictive. Beneath the brash surface, he saw glimpses of warmth that intrigued him. In the brilliance of her eyes, he found an answering attraction that encouraged him and in the flowering of her body he beheld a beauty that drew him. Proud and withdrawn, he had survived the years without a woman. His marriage had been good and he could not find it in himself to cheapen the memories with casual encounters.

Then Sara had come to live in the ranch house next door and her presence there had made him aware of the emptiness in his own home. Her goodness had appealed to him. He had felt warmed by her innocent welcome, protective of her when she was tired and vulnerable. But never had he seriously considered her available to him.

In Marcie he saw youth and beauty and a strength that had enabled her to avoid taking the easy way out of her pregnancy. She had chosen to have her child, without complaint, accepting the consequences of her own behavior, and for that he admired her.

His latest problem stood in his kitchen at this very moment, stirring something in a pot on his stove. And as he walked in the back door, Les sincerely hoped that whatever it was, it would taste better than last night's offering.

"How long do I have before dinner, Marcie?" She turned at the sound of his voice and he paused in the center of the kitchen floor. "Is there time for a shower or do I just wash up a little?"

The light over his head reflected on the silver that threaded through the hair at his temples. The harsh lines of his face were far from handsome, but Marcie thought that at this moment he was the most appealing man she had ever met. With dusty jeans and a flannel shirt that was a faded blend of red-and-black plaid, he presented a picture of solid masculine strength. The hands that rested on his hips as he watched her were large, tanned, and calloused. His jeans fit snugly over long, muscular legs, and with a start Marcie realized that she was staring at him.

"Marcie?" He moved closer and touched her shoulder. His hand lingered and his fingertips registered the tremor as she shivered beneath his touch.

"I'm sorry, Les. You startled me," she tried to explain. "Yes, you can shower before dinner." She felt the slow flush of embarrassment on her cheeks and turned her head away, reaching for the spoon that lay on the stove. "I can hold dinner . . . it's beef and noodles."

His hand lifted and he bent a bit to look past her, raising the lid of the pan. "Looks good. Have we had it before?" It did look considerably better than her usual concoctions, he realized with surprise. He caught the barely-concealed look of pleasure on her face as she registered his casual compliment. And without thinking, with no warning, his fingers caught in her hair, the soft tendrils curling around the roughness of his skin. He tugged gently, turning her face toward his. Her blue eyes were hesitant, filled with questions and for a moment he paused.

Then, before she could move, before she could speak, he fit his mouth against hers, tenderly, with such care that she forgot where she was, what she was doing, conscious only of the gentle touch that soothed her lonely heart. The spoon dropped unnoticed on the floor as she turned lithely into his body, fitting against him as if she sought shelter, her arms reaching to hold him against her, her fingers seeking purchase in the fabric of his shirt.

His response was entirely predictable and almost immediately apparent. A low, guttural laugh escaped his lips even as they lifted from hers. Without hesitation, he slid his palms down her back and held her against him, acknowledging the evidence of his arousal.

"No, don't back off, Marcie." His mouth brushed softly on hers again and she recognized the restraint in his touch. The gentle movement of his lips was soothing, even as the hard evidence of his body told her of his need. "I won't hurt you, city girl. I just want to hold you for a minute, kind of get the preliminaries out of the way between us."

Her quick intake of breath warned him of her flare of quick anger even as she twisted in his arms. "When do I get to hear about the main event?" Her voice trembled with emotion and he recognized the attempt she was making to keep her temper in check. Her nails dug fiercely into his shoulders as she tried to make space between their bodies.

"Make all the tracks you like, lady. Your fingernails are taking my mind off another problem I've got." His voice was humoring her, denying her retreat from him. His fingers worked their way up her back, holding her firmly against him and he eased the tension that he felt coiling in the muscles of her shoulders; gently, but firmly, massaging as he reluctantly shifted his body away from hers.

"You come on pretty strong, cowboy," she said, conceding agreeably. The husky murmur held a promise of humor, as her words cut the tension between them. Her temper had faded as quickly as it had arisen and his fingers slid carefully, easily from her shoulders to bury themselves in the shining fullness of her hair as he relished its curling abundance. He tugged at it easily until it escaped confinement, tightening his grip until he held her immobile, just inches from his face.

"I've been alone for a long time." His blunt admission acknowledged his need. The message in his look was clear and Marcie read the hot, searching eyes that sought an answering spark.

"I'm not here to scratch your itch, big man." Her tongue flicked over her top lip and his eyes followed its path. "I'm your babysitter and your part-time maid, Les. That's all."

His lips dropped to hers quickly, brushing against the damp trail her tongue had left and then hardened against her briefly, a last lingering taste of her mouth stolen without a trace of regret. His smile told her that he offered no apology and his words verified it.

"You're more than that . . . at least you're going to be." His mouth twisted with regret. "It would take more time than we've got to even touch my itch, little girl. When we get around to that part of it, you'll be ready." His hands dropped from her and he turned away.

Blunt and unvarnished, yet delivered with a look that was in itself a promise, his words touched a chord within her. And as a spring rainstorm washes the land, turning the grass green and cleansing the dusty residue away, so she felt the dry, bitter scales of loneliness fall from her. The harshness of his demands, the blunt sureness of him, the unyielding force of hands that had held her, and the aggressive promise he gave her spoke of a man who was thirsting for a woman's touch. He had made no secret of his attraction to her.

The time spent together during the past weeks had given her a taste of Les Cochrane that intrigued her. The years between them were unimportant, Marcie decided. He could give her security and stability, two benefits that had been lacking in her lifestyle; elements she recognized as essential to her future.

The slam of the screen door was an intrusion she welcomed as two whirlwinds of boyish exuberance burst into the kitchen. "Are we ready to eat, Marcie?" Spoken almost in unison as the dark-haired, eager faces looked up with impish glee, their words won an easy smile from her.

"Go wash up, boys. Dinner's ready." With a whoop and a short scuffle that tangled their fingers in each other's hair, they flew through the doorway. And then with the sound of the bathroom door opening, they subsided.

"Did I hear Marcie scolding you boys?" Their father's stern voice caught their attention immediately.

"No, sir." Jay spoke up quickly, the braver of the two. "She just sent us in to wash up." They scooted under his arm that stretched across the doorway and with relieved glances at each other dissolved into smothered laughter. With a tolerant shrug that escaped them, he turned away and their voices dropped to whispers, their heads together over the sink while they quickly lathered up and rinsed off the dirt that constantly accumulated on their small persons.

"Do they give you a hard time?" Les reached for the salt and pepper from the stove and Marcie quickly shook her head.

"No, Les. They're fine. I don't have a problem with either of your boys." Her glance at him was amused. "Of course, I can't say the same about their father."

His look was uncomfortable as he heard the splashing from the bathroom. "We'll talk about that later, girl . . . when we don't have an audience." The promise was implicit and she gathered it to her, the threatening look from under his brows no deterrent to her quiet happiness.

The sudden change in their relationship came as a welcome surprise to the big man who watched her so closely. He had feared that his lapse from their earlier status as employer and employee might cause problems that would present more barriers between them. Apparently the wind wasn't blowing in that direction, he thought with satisfaction as he pulled his chair from the table.

It was dark outside before she hung the dish towel to dry inside the cupboard door, and Marcie bit back a sigh as twinges of distress settled in her lower back. It's been a long day, she admitted ruefully as she rubbed long, slender fingers against the aching muscles. She cocked her head, listening. The low rumble of Les's voice from the living room told her that he was on the phone and she slipped quietly down the hallway to where he sat.

The far corner of the old parlor was his office, separated from the rest of the room by a file cabinet and bookcase. His shoulders were hunched as he bent over the open account book on his desk, one hand holding the receiver to his ear, the other rubbing distractedly at the back of his neck.

She drew closer, watching as his brown hand flexed, ruffling the dark hair that curled at his nape. Her eyes followed the movement, helplessly admiring the muscles that tensed, pulling the worn shirt across his back . . . remembering the touch of those calloused fingertips against her skin. She inhaled sharply at the direction of her thoughts and his head jerked up. He twisted in his chair, mumbled a quick excuse into the telephone, and leaned back, his eyes assessing her keenly.

"You look tired, girl."

"Just a little." The admission was a lie. She reconsidered and shrugged in an attempt to pacify his concern. "Maybe more than a little, Les. I didn't sleep well last night . . . maybe tonight will make up for it." She backed away from him, turning to leave the room and he rose, his movements abrupt as he caught her hand before she could make good her escape.

"Are you working too hard here?"

Her eyes met his quickly and her head shook in answer. "No, don't think that. It's just me, I mean the fact that I'm . . ." Her voice trailed off as her hand automatically moved to touch the mound beneath her loose T-shirt.

"I know what you mean," he drawled softly and his gaze dropped to where she touched. "I've lived through two pregnancies with my wife, Marcie. I'm no stranger to your condition." His hand released hers and lifted to smooth wispy tendrils of hair from her cheek. "I've always had a thing for pregnant ladies. They bring out the gentleman in me." His eyes were slow in their appraisal, hesitating as they paid silent approval to the firm lift of her breasts and then rising to meet her own. He brushed his fingers across her mouth, a casual caress that brought her warm, unexpected pleasure.

"I warn you, Marcie. I won't always be a gentleman with you. Be thinking about it, will you?"

"Thinking about what?" Her voice sounded high, uneven, and breathless.

"I don't need to tell you, girl. You know I want you here with me. You've known it for weeks. I can take care of you . . . and your baby." His pause was deliberate. "Just think about it, okay?"

He dipped his head slowly and carefully. This kiss lacked tenderness and delicacy, but what it lacked it made up for in the message it delivered. His hands gripped her shoulders and he drew her nearer, their bodies barely touching as he branded her with his desire, the touch of their lips brief but deliberate. His, open and hot against her softness; hers, opening hesitantly. He broke the contact and stepped back.

"I'll see you tomorrow afternoon. I hope you sleep better tonight." A grin lit his eyes with an unfamiliar mischief. "Dream about me, will you?"

Her thoughts were tumbled and distracted as she drove the short distance back to the Hyatt ranch. But her dreams as she lay sleeping hours later were focused entirely on the image of a dark-haired man with gentle hands.

TEN

Sara's toes searched the floor next to the bed for the terry slippers she had kicked off last night and she shrugged into her robe, eyes still half-closed and sleep lines creased into her cheek. Cal thought he had never seen her more vulnerable and appealing. He stood in the doorway watching her while she tied the belt and then scraped her hair back with both hands, pulling the unruly curls to hang behind her shoulders. Her mouth opened and her hand covered the yawn that escaped just as she caught sight of the man leaning in the doorway, his eyes warm with unexpected affection as they met hers.

"You don't look ready to get up yet, Sara. Bad night?" His tone was teasing and he expected the faint flush that stained her cheeks as she tipped her chin up and held his gaze. Her memories of the night were far from bad and well he knew it, she thought.

"I managed to suffer through it." Only the twitch of her lips betrayed her humor and with two long steps Cal was upon her, his hands bold and searching as he pulled her against him, her back tight against the warmth of his body. His fingers eased open the knot in the belt that fit snugly about her waist and she leaned easily against him as he parted the robe and touched her with arousing familiarity through the thin gown she wore.

His lips were buried in the tender spot beneath her ear and she lost her dignity as she heard the words he growled, working his way around to her throat, tipping her head back, and finally turning her in his embrace to better locate her mouth. She eased her arms between their bodies and curled them about his neck, pulling his head down, inviting his touch.

Here in the privacy of their room, she had come to find a haven that filled the secret places in her heart. His embrace had become a sanctuary for her and she waited impatiently each night for him to slide into bed with her. Waited quietly, stilling her restlessness, until he turned to her with open arms and she could once more seek the security of his body, folded protectively about her. She felt silent tears creep from her eyes sometimes as her heart overflowed with the love she longed to express. Her lips had formed the words more than once, she had whispered them silently into his flesh, and into the crisp curls that she loved to bury her face in as he nuzzled the tender spot between her breasts.

"I love you!" They came to her so easily and hovered on her lips. Perhaps he had heard them whispered in the night, she decided, and had ignored them, not wanting to embarrass her by his lack of response. Through the months she had come to the conclusion that Cal gave her all that he could. When the time came that he found love in his heart for her, he would tell her. If that time never came, she would be satisfied with what she had with him.

"Mmmm . . ." His soft growl of appreciation was muffled against her warmth and he lifted his head to eye her. A wicked grin curled his lips and his tongue tucked itself slyly into the corner of his mouth.

"I'd like to settle for breakfast in bed this morning," he suggested softly.

Sara wiggled against him, deciding that he was more than half serious. But then he straightened and shook his head slowly, his mouth brushing across her forehead with each motion. His words were spaced between the soft kisses that spoke their own language.

"Sweetheart? Bess has breakfast ready for us. Bacon and eggs . . . toast and coffee. I don't suppose we'd better let it get cold."

The words set her stomach churning. Eggs were not her favorite thing to eat anyway, but she usually obliged Bess by stuffing them down, scrambled or soft boiled, at least twice a week. She stirred against him restlessly and stepped back.

"I think just a piece of toast for me, Cal." A wobbly smile touched her lips as his hands reluctantly released her. "I'll be right down. Let me comb my hair and wash my face."

She turned away toward the bathroom and his eyes betrayed a trace of concern as he watched her go. Her face had looked drawn lately, she had seemed pale and tired last night. His conscience told him that it had not been fair to Sara to haul her here, turn her into a ranch wife, and let her work at it with such determination. But he knew that his protests would fall on deaf ears. Sara was stubborn. Her pride in her ability to cope with his household was enormous and he drew silent satisfaction from her efforts to make his life more comfortable.

"I'll be downstairs." His voice drifted to her through

the bathroom door. She stood before the mirror, frowning at the freckles that stood out so prominently against her wan features. This light sure isn't very flattering, I look like the very dickens, she decided and then bent to splash warm water over her cheeks. Her hairbrush made quick work of the curling confusion that framed her face and she pulled it back into a tortoise-shell clasp at the nape of her neck.

"That's better." With another critical glance in the mirror, she straightened the collar of her robe and turned up the sleeves. The smell of coffee wafted up the stairway as she ran down to the kitchen and wrinkled her nose. Nothing appealed to her this morning.

"You didn't eat much, missy." Bess took her plate from the table and eyed her with barely-concealed worry.

"Sorry, Bess." Sara ducked her head and lifted her shoulders in silent apology. Her smile came easily and Bess capitulated to the charm of the girl who had become so dear to her. In a last attempt to coax her, she turned back from the sink.

"How about a blueberry muffin, then." They were warm and fragrant and very tempting as the older woman lifted the plate and offered it for Sara's inspection.

"Hmmm . . . maybe I will." She chose carefully, aiming for the one with the most plump, purple berries visible through the golden surface.

"Boy, does that look good!" Marcie came through the doorway and reached to snatch a muffin from the plate as she passed it. She sniffed at it and closed her eyes. "Smells wonderful, Bess."

The heartfelt praise brought a grudging smile to her face as Bess considered the young woman. Marcie was beginning to show promise, she thought. She'll never be the woman that Sara is, her loyal heart declared, but she might turn out all right yet.

Les Cochrane was probably the best thing that had ever happened to her. That sage conclusion had been formed over the past weeks as she watched Marcie be transformed from a careless, impudent girl to the woman who now had taken on the running of their neighbor's household. She had spent hours with the two little boys who were in her care—hours during which an obvious affection had developed among them. The three of them had formed a rare friendship and Les's children were thriving under the influence of Marcie's budding maternal instincts. Her feelings toward Les were more concealed, but . . . Bess smiled secretly. Changes were in the offing at the ranch next door, if she knew anything about men and women!

Marcie was spending long minutes on her morning coffee, measuring sugar and cream deliberately, watching Sara from beneath lowered brows, and picking carefully at the paper that contained her breakfast, peeling the pleated covering away and eating the crumbs as they fell.

"Are they worth a penny?" Sara's teasing broke in and with a short laugh Marcie nodded.

"I've been sitting here wondering how much you've figured out by yourself."

"Not much really . . ." Sara fingered the napkin she had folded several times, waiting for her friend to continue.

"I like him, you know." The admission felt good. Like a ray of sunshine, her smile radiated, lighting her eyes with such pure happiness that Sara felt her throat thicken with tears. It had been years since she had seen that expression on Marcie's face. The cynical half-smile seldom appeared any longer. The lost, lonely look that had haunted Sara's thoughts of her friend had been transformed into a quiet expression of contentment. Even her occasional grumblings about Les's boys and her near failures at cooking were just final whimpers of defiance at her changing lifestyle.

"I suspect the feeling is mutual, if my opinion is being asked." Her words were heartfelt. "You deserve something good in your life, Marcie. Les is a fine man. You couldn't do much better if you set out looking for one."

"I guess that's how I feel, too, about Les I mean. But I have to admit I'm glad that you agree with me. I've always valued your opinion, Sara." She shifted uneasily in her chair for a moment, seeking a more comfortable position as the baby stretched within her. A grimace touched her face as she rubbed her palms slowly in small circles against her belly, almost unconscious of her actions.

Sara watched with hungry eyes. "Does it bother you when the baby moves? Do you mind it?" Her questions had been infrequent but as Marcie's body grew progressively larger, she had been more aware of the toll her pregnancy was taking.

Her hands stilled and Marcie closed her eyes, a small smile of contentment giving Sara her answer. "Not really, just once in a while when he pokes me in my ribs." She glanced up and caught the yearning expression that Sara wore.

"Have you thought about having a baby?"

"Not really . . . not for a while, anyway." She looked away and Marcie caught a glimpse of uncertainty beneath the smile that brought swift anger to her voice.

"Doesn't Cal like the idea? Or are you afraid to ask him about it?"

"No, that isn't it." She turned back quickly, shaking her head in denial. Her mouth lifted again in a mocking grin. "I'll wait till you have yours before I bring it up. I suspect you'll need all the help you can get and I'm sure I can use a little practice with babies before I decide to start one of my own." Satisfied that she had dispelled Marcie's criticism of Cal, Sara rose from the table and then turned back momentarily as she remembered the question she had posed a few moments ago.

"Is the feeling mutual, Marcie?"

"How can you really tell?" Confusion clouded her face and she shook her head slowly, her indecision apparent. "He's different than any man I've ever known, Sara." Slowly, she searched for words that would express the uncertainty of her thoughts. "He needs me, or at least he needs someone. Maybe any woman would do . . . in fact, I'm sure a lot of women would be able to do a better job than I am." She smiled ruefully. "We both know that my cooking skills leave much to be desired, but he doesn't seem to mind." Her thoughts skittered about and she tried to put into words the turmoil that had churned through her dreams all night long.

"How can I tell if it's me he likes, Sara? Or just the fact that he has someone there to look after the boys, someone who is available. Not that I'm very appealing right now. Although . . ." she remembered suddenly what Les had said to her and her eyes sparkled with humor. "He told me last night that he had a thing for pregnant ladies." She stood and spread her arms wide, turning in place in a slow circle, and then came to a halt, once more facing Sara.

"Can you believe that he honestly thinks this is sexy?"

Her head bobbed up and down and she reached to hug Marcie with enthusiasm, laughing delightedly. "I believe it . . . I believe it!" The baby moved between them and Sara froze in place, her mood transformed in an instant. "Oh, Marcie, that's exciting." Her response to the firm movement of Marcie's unborn child was unexpected. For a few seconds she felt a sharp, piercing stab of envy that surprised her and in a moment she turned away in confusion.

The approach of Thanksgiving brought a surge of energy to the household. Bess hummed under her breath as she readied pecans and pumpkin to fill the pie shells she had prepared. Marcie furiously scanned the cookbook for a stuffing recipe that did not require the use of cornbread. And Sara fought an attack of nausea and weakness that threatened to ruin her day. Cal was in rare good humor, apparently in tune with the undercurrents that had put a sparkle in Marcie's eyes. The thought that she might soon be moving to the Cochrane ranch, bag and baggage, was enough to give him a new lease on life, he thought.

"Sara . . ." His murmur was coaxing in her ear as he roused her from the half-sleep that had claimed her at sunrise. She smiled at the whisper of his breath against her skin and kept her eyes closed, waiting. His mouth moved again against her earlobe and the suggestion he made bordered on being risque.

"Cal! Are you serious? Everyone must be up by now!" She sat up abruptly and then wished she hadn't as bile rose in her throat. His long arm reached to tug at her gown.

"Come here, honey. Just give me a little snuggle,

will you?'' He pulled her down easily into his arms and gathered her closer. His hand massaged lightly against her back and she sighed with pleasure as she nestled into his warmth. The uneasiness in her stomach faded as she closed her eyes for a moment, relaxing against him.

"Sara?" His whisper was a question.

"Ummm . . ." She lifted her face and her mouth touched his in silent agreement.

"Thought you were going to sleep all day." Delivered in a gruff tone, Bess's accusation fell on deaf ears. Cal was in a holiday mood today and nothing would change that. He pulled the string on his housekeeper's apron and casually ignored the dish towel that flew in his direction.

"What's this doing on the floor?" Sara stepped over it and bent to pick up the striped terrycloth as she entered the kitchen, still rosy from the quick shower she had taken. Her hair hung in damp ringlets down her back and the shine on her face was not entirely due to soap and water, if Bess had things figured out correctly.

"Bess dropped it." Cal had his head buried in the newspaper and his response was bland and innocent. Sara looked doubtfully at the two of them: Bess busy at the stove, her apron undone; and Cal seated at the table, looking at her now over the top of the paper, his eyes warm and admiring.

"Want some coffee?" he offered.

She shook her head and went to the refrigerator, bent to locate the orange juice, and then found two glasses in the cupboard. "Not this morning, Cal. I still don't feel right. Must be the pizza we made last night." She poured the juice and offered a glass to Bess.

"Have you had breakfast yet?" Sara peered past Bess's shoulder at the stove. "What are you cooking?"

"Just put the giblets on to simmer for a while so I can put them in the gravy later on." She slid the pan to a back burner and lifted a skillet from a hook over the stove. "I'm ready to do bacon and eggs now. Place your orders." She took the juice glass from Sara's hand and drank it quickly. "Thanks, missy . . . Mr. Cal didn't have juice yet either."

Sara reached to the table and deposited the other glass in front of Cal and turned back to Bess. "You didn't tie your apron this morning. Let me do it." Her fingers were busy at the task and she missed the smile that was exchanged over her head.

Breakfast was barely cleared away when Sara heard car doors slamming and voices raised in greeting. The masculine sounds brought her to attention and the barely-concealed glee on Bess's face alerted her.

Her eyes lit with delight. "Do I sense a conspiracy?" Sudden recognition of a booming bass outside the house put wings to Sara's feet and she flew headlong out the back door . . . only to be caught up in a pair of strong arms that threatened to squeeze the breath from her lungs.

"Patrick!" Her squeal of greeting brought an answering chorus as three more O'Briens closed in on the reunion. Lost in the huddle of masculinity, Sara turned from one to another of her family, bestowing hugs and kisses without hesitation, until the face of her beloved father was before her.

"Oh, Daddy! I've missed you." Her heartfelt cry touched the emotions of the man who watched the reunion, and Cal knew deep satisfaction at the success of his Thanksgiving Day surprise for his wife.

It had taken just a five-minute phone call to set the

wheels in motion and Sara's delight made him wonder why he had not issued the invitation months ago. As if she sensed his presence, she turned from her father's arms and Cal found himself the recipient of her gratitude as she clung to him shamelessly in front of family and hired hands alike. The noises of welcome had brought the men from the barn and they watched with satisfaction as Cal held his wife in a close embrace.

"Are you pleased?" The question was after the fact and Cal knew it but he asked anyway. The flurry of kisses that answered him brought a flush to his cheekbones and he set Sara on her feet quickly. "Whoa, girl . . . simmer down here." His chuckle brought Sara back from euphoria and she looked about with startled eyes.

"Oh my . . . I did get carried away, didn't I?" She laughed aloud. "But I don't care . . . I'm so happy, Cal."

She reached for her brothers' hands and towed Patrick and Dennis behind her as she headed for the back porch. "Come on inside . . . all of you." The invitation floated over her shoulder as she went and with a shrug and a grin of acceptance her brothers followed.

A fresh pot of coffee was put on to brew and news of home was welcomed by Sara as she quizzed the men who surrounded her. And then they asked their own questions and she eagerly took them on a tour of her home, proudly pointing out the evidence of her attempts at homemaking, ever conscious of Cal in the background, quietly approving as he watched.

Cal's suggestions of a ride across the closest pastures was accepted with enthusiasm and he left the house, his brothers-in-law and Sara's father close behind. Horses were saddled and bridled and a line of riders headed out to inspect Sara's new home, Cameron O'Brien riding with Cal at the front of the group.

"Haven't done this in years, Cal," the older man admitted as he adjusted his body in the saddle. "Back in the old days, my folks had a farm west of town. We used to ride a lot, but mostly bareback." He shifted again. "I'm counting on this being a short ride though, or I may be eating dinner on my feet."

"We won't go far," Cal said with an agreeable grin as he waited for the three brothers to catch up.

"I don't know how you got us talked into this, Cal." Jonathan's expression was wary. "Are you sure this is a good idea?"

"You've got the quietest horse in my barn between your legs, little brother." Cal fought hard to contain his amusement at the look of discomfort on Sara's brother's face.

"Little brother . . . did you hear that, Patrick?" Jonathan chuckled as he looked about him and Sara laughed in delight as the teasing words drifted back to where she stood, watching the riders as they formed a group around her husband.

She had been delighted at the easy acquiescence of her father and brothers when they heard Cal's offer of a ride. Now, she lifted her hand to wave at them, but they were caught up in their mock conflict and in a moment were out of sight, over a rise in the pasture. She turned back to the house and Bess and the preparation of what promised to be a day filled with thanksgiving.

Long before five o'clock the scent of roasting turkey filled the house and had drifted into the yard. Their appetites aroused by the aroma, the men in the bunkhouse headed for the back porch and by the time dinner was announced they were waiting, having been joined by Sara's three brothers. Leaning on the upright posts and slouched against the railing, they were ready, their indolent postures a sham. When Sara opened the screen door and announced with a smile that dinner was ready, only their innate courtesy saved her from a stampede.

She moved ahead of them, escorting the noisy group into the dining room, where Cal and her father were giving Bess a hand. The huge turkey sat at one end of the table. Large bowls held vegetables, gravy, stuffing, and various salads, bringing huge grins to the faces of the men who had seldom seen a Thanksgiving feast of this dimension.

Sara was delighted with their response to her masterpiece. Bess had graciously accepted all of the suggestions offered, agreeing to the vast assortment of dishes Sara had decided on. Turkey and stuffing with potatoes and maybe a dish of beans had been the usual holiday fare at this table, but Cal's wife had brought her own ideas with her when she moved in. Her idea of holidays was a shade different than what they were used to, but Cal and Bess were more than agreeable when it came to pleasing Sara.

"Boy, have we missed you, Sara," Dennis announced between bites.

"And what's wrong with my cooking?" Jonathan asked. A chorus of male voices answered and her youngest brother looked at Sara appealingly. "See the abuse I take, sis?" He shook his head in mock distress.

Sara looked about her table and felt her heart overflow with delight. "I'm so glad you're all here," she said with a voice that held a whisper of the tears she felt crowding her throat. She bestowed a look of benevolence on Jonathan. "I'll even give you a few tips that might help your reputation in the kitchen before you leave,'' she offered, willing away the bittersweet emotion that gripped her.

She had watched with pleasure as everyone found their seats and then bowed their heads for the blessing. Cal spoke the same words his father had prayed before him, unknowingly using the same inflections of speech and bringing tears to the eyes of Bess as she remembered other Thanksgiving dinners around this table. And then with little ceremony, the food was eaten and approved of as Bess and Sara saw their morning's work devoured. She watched in amazement as the men tackled the pies, eating a piece of each kind, while she valiantly struggled to finish the small sliver of pecan she had taken.

"Thank you, ma'am. . . ." The words echoed in her ears as she helped clear up the dishes and watched as the hands left to finish up evening chores. Even with a holiday, the animals required attention and though everyone had spent most of the day as they wanted to, she knew it would be an hour before Cal returned to the house.

"Keep your family inside, Sara," Cal instructed. "They need a chance to have you to themselves for a while." And so she did, caught up in the familiar repartee that had been so much a part of her life in Goose Creek.

The noise from the dining room carried to the yard and Marcie tugged at Les as she hurried him toward the welcome sound.

"Sara, are you here?" Marcie's voice caught her attention and Sara welcomed her as she heard the screen door slam shut.

"In the dining room, Marcie." Her smile was contagious as she turned to greet the couple who stood in the doorway. Les, his arm draped across Marcie's shoulders possessively, looked about at the gathering of men who, without exception, were staring at Marcie with varying expressions of questioning surprise.

"Any coffee left?" Stepping away from him, Marcie slipped into a dining room chair, surveyed the group seated about the table and announced blithely, "Surprise, fellas! Marcie's in town." With barely a flick of her eyelashes, she reached for Les's hand and he stepped behind her chair, his fingers lightly clasping her shoulders.

"This is Les," she said quietly and proudly. Her forefinger pointed to each man in turn as she made the introductions. "You are about to meet Sara's family, Les. This is Patrick, Jonathan next, Mr. O'Brien at the end, and the big one beside him is Dennis." She watched in silence as each man in turn stood and stretched across the table to clasp the hand of the man who stood near her. He nodded and repeated each name and then turned to Sara.

"How did a little thing like you get into this bunch?" he teased. "How are you, Sara?"

"I'm just fine, Les. This has been a wonderful day." She turned to Marcie and they exchanged looks of mutual pleasure.

"Hasn't it, though," Marcie agreed with a pleased grin and then leaned her head back and sighed. "The only problem was that I didn't know that cooking a dinner like that would wear me out!"

"How was the turkey?" Sara asked. "Did the dressing come out all right?"

Marcie grimaced a bit and raised an eyebrow, but Les shook his head at her. "It was fine, Sara. Next year will be even better, once Marcie gets the hang of it." He sat down in the chair next to his cook and placed his hat on the table next to him. "I may even let her practice a little at Christmas time, if she behaves herself."

The rare teasing from Les Cochrane was an eye-opener, Sara thought. His eyes were warm on Marcie, his hand hovered over hers where it rested in her lap, and Sara sensed a shift in the relationship that brought a speculative look to her eye. Marcie had been surprisingly reticent about Les lately, her usual exuberance and flighty attitude with men had done a complete turn-around this time.

"The real reason I made Les bring me over so soon after dinner is . . ." Marcie hesitated, embarrassed, glaring at Les as he dipped his head to hide a grin. She shrugged finally and confessed. "My pies weren't fit to eat. Les said that something must have been wrong with the recipe I used."

His sober nod vied with the twinkle in his eyes as the rancher agreed with her. "You might say that was the problem, all right." He nodded his thanks as Sara set a cup of coffee before him and paused to pour some for Marcie.

"In that case, I don't suppose I could coax you to try some of ours, could I?" She approached the table again, this time with plates and forks ready. "Bess," she raised her voice, turning toward the kitchen. "Have we any pie left?"

With a pie plate in each hand, Bess came through the doorway. "Not much, just two pumpkin and one pecan. About enough for an evening snack, I expect."

"Save me a little for breakfast," a masculine voice pleaded behind her as Cal followed Bess through into the dining room. He nodded briefly at Les and Marcie and sat down next to where Sara stood. One large, brown hand snaked up to grasp her wrist and he tugged her closer, establishing his claim. Even the presence of her family could not entirely eliminate the faint pangs of jealousy that still stabbed at him when he saw Sara near the other man, even on an occasion as innocent as this one. He felt a possessive need to keep her near, an impulse to make her freshly aware of the narrow gold band she wore on her left hand.

Sara's eyes were soft and knowing as she glanced at him and her lips curved in a reassuring smile that pleased him. The talk around the table had easily shifted to a casual questioning of Marcie, and Sara watched and listened as her brothers teased Marcie about her retreat from New York. That they did not mention her obvious pregnancy was a credit to their upbringing, Sara thought, even as she realized that she would face their quizzing later.

Les cleared his throat to gain attention and laid down his fork. "I know this is a family occasion, but I thought you might like to know about some plans Marcie and I have made today." All eyes were upon him as he continued. "We've about decided to make some permanent arrangements at my house." His eyes warmed as they rested on the woman next to him. "Marcie has about agreed to take on the job of me and my boys."

Like a shot, Sara was out of her chair, around the table and had her arms outstretched. With a small cry of gladness, Marcie met her and the two friends shared an embrace that brought final healing to the differences that had marred their friendship. "Thank you, Sara." The words were whispered in her ear and Sara's nod acknowledged them. They separated reluctantly, both of them blinking back tears that would not be denied.

"I understand why Marcie is bawling, since she's going to be stuck with Les Cochrane, but what on earth is your problem, Sara?" Cal rested his hands on her waist as he teased her and Sara turned from Marcie to smile at him as she wiped quickly at her face.

She sniffed and drew a sigh that signaled her forebearance with him. "You couldn't be expected to understand, Cal. Being a mere man is such a handicap."

Nothing could mar the evening now, he thought. Sara could get in her licks if she liked. Marcie could stick around for a while, now that he was sure she would be gone before long. And even Cochrane was off his list. Having her family here today had been good for Sara. Life in his household was going to be back on an even keel and he had the feeling that all would be right with his world before long.

And then Sara's eldest brother spoke. "Someone else is getting married, Sara. I forgot to tell you . . . Tom asked Julie Benson and she said yes. Sure surprised everybody," Patrick announced. His eyes teased her as he whispered across the table, "He finally got over you, little sister."

"Patrick!" Sara admonished him crossly as she glanced at Cal. His lips had tightened at Patrick's careless words, but he relaxed with an effort he could not hide from Sara and smiled casually at her. She felt a censure that puzzled her, but it was not until the house was settled down for the night that she discovered its source.

"Who is Tom?" The harsh tone of his voice told Sara that Cal had dropped his facade of pleasantry and she closed her eyes rather than face his bleak countenance.

"Please, Cal. Don't spoil today," she pleaded quietly. But he would not be put off and he pulled her to face him, his hands hard against her softness.

Her face was in shadow as he loomed over her, and she felt curiously vulnerable beneath his bulk. She shivered against his warmth and opened her eyes. The look of confused unhappiness she wore tore at his defenses. Cal loosened his hold and his hands became soothing against her flesh. So pleased was she by his about-face that she was stunned by the question he asked.

"Was Tom the one, Sara?"

Her abrupt retreat took him by surprise and she was standing beside the bed before he could grasp her intent. He watched her, saw the sadness engulf her expression, and immediately regretted the words he had spoken. But it was too late.

"Tom was a friend, Cal. Patrick's friend and mine. I dated him a few times . . . and yes, he wanted me. But he never had me." Her mouth twisted and her jaw clenched as she fought for control. "Will you never be able to forget?" She shook her head as if she answered her own question. "Will I always be on trial with you?"

"Sara . . ." he began, but she turned away and he was still as he watched her walk across the room. She sank down into the chair that sat by the window and wrapped her arms about herself as if to stave off the chill in the air.

"If there was another place to sleep tonight . . . if the house weren't full," she began, and Cal broke in before her sentence could be completed.

"You're not leaving this bedroom, Sara. I don't care how angry you are with me, this is where you belong." He had approached her as he spoke and she looked up at him warily.

"I'm not angry, Cal. I just feel empty . . . and a little sad, I guess." She lifted her hands to him in a gesture of defeat. "I'm not angry," she repeated. "It's just that I feel a breach between us and I thought we would be better off apart for a few hours."

Without dignifying her stand with a denial, Cal

leaned over, lifting her and holding her close to his chest. "I'm sorry, Sara." His apology was spoken into her hair, his breath ruffling the curls at her temple. "Don't threaten to leave our bed, please. I don't want to have to chase you through the house, and believe me, I will if you try to sleep somewhere else." In three easy steps he had carried her to the bed and in seconds he had lowered her to the sheet. He never released his hold on her as he settled himself next to her and covered them both. Then he snuggled her next to him, easing her gown up as he shifted his position, until he had stripped the cotton fabric from her and tossed it to the floor.

"Cal!" Her single word of protest went unanswered as he turned to her for reassurance. And then she murmured another word, one that pleased him and caused him to chuckle beneath his breath.

"Do you like that, Sara?" His whisper followed the curves of her breasts and his mouth pressed with hot, damp kisses against the silken softness of her skin.

In the silent shiver of her response, he found satisfaction. In the quiet embrace of her arms, he found delight. And in the long hours of the night, he discovered a depth of passion within himself that strengthened the chains that bound him to the girl he held within his embrace.

ELEVEN

"Are you happy, girl?" The question hung between them and Cameron O'Brien watched his daughter closely. Expressions chased across her face. She looked, he thought, both uncertain and yet like a woman in love. She was blooming, there was no doubt about that, and his heart was reassured by the way her husband watched after her.

Cam clasped her hand between both of his and it was lost there. The gentle hands of her father had held Sara's many times in the past. In fact, some of her fondest memories of childhood involved the hands of Cameron O'Brien.

Pushing her swing high in the air, until she was breathless and gasping with happy laughter, his hands would then catch the wooden seat, slowing her until she came to a stop. His sturdy palms clasped about her waist, while he lifted her high over his head, swinging her in a circle, laughing with her, teasing her in a loving way, until she wrapped her arms about his neck and clung like a limpet to a rock.

"Oh, Daddy, I love you!" How many times she had

told him over the years, how many times his big, calloused hands had held his daughter, how many memories she had stockpiled against the time when memories
might be all she would have of the father she loved so
dearly. But for now, he was here. For now, she had
the reality of the only parent she really remembered.
The faint echo of the past that was her mother was only
a memory—wispy bits of treasured moments that came
to mind like fragments of a dream.

And now he had asked her a question. Knowing that
she owed him the truth, she hesitated. And in that
moment of hesitation, she became aware that the simple
truth was easy to speak.

"Yes, Daddy. Yes, I'm happy."

His lined face brightened and his smile was a beauty
to behold. Her own matched it and together they turned
away from the house, their clasped hands swinging
between them as they walked down the dusty driveway.

"It's not always wonderful, Daddy." She felt the
need to be honest, as honest as she could be without
betraying confidences that belonged to her marriage
. . . that were private and secret and a part of her life
with Cal. But the life they led together on this ranch
was open for discussion and she wanted Cameron to
share it with her.

"Some days I work hard, Cal works hard, and the
weather is hot, and someone gets hurt or machinery
breaks down somewhere. Those are the days when I
feel down in the dumps or discouraged and cranky. But
it doesn't take much to pick me up . . . usually just a
hug and a kiss, if the truth be known." She slanted a
glance at him and Cameron caught the glint of humor
that glowed from her expressive face.

"Ah, he's got you pegged, lass. I knew a good man
would soon figure out how to handle you." He paused

for a moment, as the autumn sun warmed them in its rays, and took stock of his daughter. She was slender, more so than ever in her adult life, but she looked fulfilled, content. And for that he was thankful. She appeared fragile, but he knew she had the strength inherited from her Irish mother. She was beautiful, within and without . . . but more than that, she glowed with the inherent goodness that had been given to her by the parents who had loved each other so well; And who, in turn, had shared that love with their children. He was satisfied. His girl-child was thriving in this place where her love had led her, and Cameron O'Brien was pleased.

"Daddy, don't get me wrong," she said slowly. "There are bad days, but most of them are good." She looked up at the lined face above her and her smile was pure and honest. "Cal is good to me, Daddy . . . and I love him." Her smile dimmed, just a bit. In fact, if he had not been so attuned to her mood, Cam might have missed the faint difference in her glowing face. Then she grinned and he answered her with a hug that threatened to squeeze her beyond breathing.

"I love you, girl . . . I truly do," he declared. "And so does that young man of yours."

For just a moment, her eyes flickered from his. "Do you think so, Daddy?" And then she flitted from him and turned in a circle before him, preening as if she stood before a mirror. "Of course, he does. How could he help it, with me so gorgeous and all!"

And then she faltered and swayed, and if it had not been for the steadying hand of her father, she might have sat down in the dusty driveway. She blinked and shook her head and grinned up at him, recovering quickly. "I got dizzy, spinning around like that. I'd better act my age, hadn't I?"

The walk to the mailbox by the road proceeded at a slower pace and Sara clung to her father's hand as they reminisced together.

The weekend passed in a flurry of riding, walking, and teasing conversation that involved Cal to the utmost. By Sunday afternoon, when the late-model sedan pulled away bearing her family, Sara felt that the time had been well spent. For the first time in her marriage, she was rock-bottom content. No longer lonesome for the loved ones she had missed, no sense of longing for the small town she had sprung from. She felt at home here. Here with Cal, Bess, and the men who helped run this ranch. Especially, she felt content with Cal.

But content was not the word to describe Cal's mood. Sara watched through sleepy eyes as he stripped his shirt off and dropped it across the hamper. His movements were crisp and measured, as if he performed this ritual for her benefit. Her smile came slowly and though he appeared to be engrossed in his nightly routine, she sensed his awareness of her.

With a raspy, metallic sound, he loosened his jeans and then sat on the edge of a sturdy wooden chair to tug at his boots. His flesh glistened warmly in the glow of the lamplight and his hair gleamed with streaks of golden brilliance throughout the paler sun-bleached curls.

He's mine, she thought. As if he sensed her possessive announcement, he looked up and their eyes met in flaring recognition. Deliberately, fully aware of her scrutiny, he stood, carrying his boots to the closet, then bent to place them side by side on the floor. Standing erect, he lowered his jeans and without taking his gaze from her, dropped them to the carpet and stepped free.

Sara's fingers gathered the top hem of the sheet and

drew it down and toward her, uncovering the space where Cal would sleep tonight. She tugged his pillow into place and moved it a few inches closer to her own. As if it were a ritual, she readied the bed for him and he watched her, silent and still, only his eyes moving as he followed the path of her agile fingers. Her mouth pursed as she lifted her head and considered him and her eyes narrowed with appraisal.

"You don't look sleepy any more, Mrs. Hyatt." His hands were on his hips now and his thumbs edged beneath the elastic band of the white briefs he wore.

"Don't I?" The question was accompanied by a slow smile and he was fascinated by the pouting softness.

"Saving that place for anybody special, ma'am?" he was closer now, his voice a husky giveaway as his body betrayed his arousal.

He leaned closer and swept the sheet from her just as her arms rose to greet him. "Cal . . ." Her foolish game was at an end. His nearness brought to life the passion that he had nurtured so carefully. Her trust in him was complete, her body responded of its own volition and as he knelt beside her and felt the strength of her embrace, he sensed her surrender.

"Cal . . . I . . ." The words went unspoken as he lowered his head and took possession of her lips. He captured her whispered sounds of pleasure, his mouth tasting the sweetness of her breath. "Ah, Cal." Her words were a gentle caress to his ears and he whispered softly against her lips.

"What, baby? What do you want?" The flame of his arousal burned higher and he clamped down on the persistent throbbing that pushed him to take her quickly.

"Just you, Cal," she whispered in invitation. Her eyes were no longer heavy, they opened wide to meet his and the brilliant green glow that told him of her need fed his own. Her smile was sultry, her lips still wet from his kiss, her teeth gleaming and parted and the tip of her tongue tempted him as it skittered across her top lip. Tempting, warm, wet, and waiting—she lay before him and he accepted her invitation.

With a groan that told her of the desire and passion he could not voice aloud, he reached for her. With hands that could have bruised her, he brought her instead to flaming readiness, his touch always sensitive to her woman's flesh. With hot kisses that branded her, he claimed her as his own . . . and with careful, deliberate movements he carried her with him to a completion that stunned her with its beauty.

She lay within his arms and felt the shuddering of his breathing as he rested against her and her fingers clasped him as if she could hold him closer. As if she must cling to him, as if her skin craved the touch of his . . . she held tightly to him. And as her mouth brushed against his throat, her whispered words of love sounded as the brush of angel's wings in his ears.

"Marcie didn't come home last night." Bess's announcement met Sara as she entered the kitchen and the flat tones of the older woman's voice warned her of Bess's disapproval.

"She's must have stayed at Les's place," Sarah said as she headed for the refrigerator. She opened the door and searched for the orange juice.

"Do you suppose we'll ever want turkey again?" She shuddered visibly as she viewed the remains of the enormous bird they had all but demolished at the dinner table several days before. "I can't face turkey leftovers, Bess." Sara reached for a glass and poured her orange juice, then leaned against the cupboard as she drank it.

Bess turned from the stove and viewed Sara with a

frown. "Don't change the subject, girl. If Les and Mar-cie want to spend their nights together, they need to get married first. And you know it."

"But we don't know how together they are, do we?" Sara felt the need to defend Marcie, but Bess would not be appeased so easily.

"All I know is that when Mr. Cal wanted to live with a woman, he went out and got her and brought her home with a ring on her finger." As if that were the final word on the subject, Bess turned away.

"They're going to get married, Bess. Probably right away, in fact." At least I hope so, Sara thought, unwilling to express any doubt on the matter aloud.

"You really want to marry me?" Her words held more than a thread of hope and Marcie waited for the reassurance she needed.

"Didn't you believe me, Marcie? I thought I made it clear what my intentions were when we went to the Hyatt's after dinner Thursday." Les approached her as she stood at the back door. She had determined to make a quick exit this morning. In fact, it had been a hassle to get the boys breakfast out of the way, both of them determined to grab a handful of cookies and run with them. Her conscience nudging her, she was on her way to visit Sara. But first she wanted to establish her posi-tion in Les's life.

The fact that he wanted her was in itself a minor miracle, as far as she was concerned. His arms about her yesterday had been warm and comforting . . . for a few minutes. Until his lips brushed against hers in a caress that gave his embrace new meaning.

The rough exterior of Les Cochrane covered a sensi-tive man who had made her more aware than ever before that she was a desirable woman—that her pregnancy was no deterrent to his wanting her. He had adjusted with practiced ease to the rounding of her belly and his hand had slid down, to rest with possessive fingers spread across her stomach. The faint movement beneath his hand brought a satisfied smile to his lips and he closed his eyes as he concentrated, waiting to feel the tiny hands or feet move inside her body.

He had been explicit in his choice of words as he vowed his intentions to her. "This will be our child, Marcie. I don't care who the man is who put it there . . ." His fingers moved slowly in a circle as he circumscribed the area where her child lay hidden.

"It will be ours. I'm going to be its father and it's going to be legal." His words were slow and precise and she bowed her head as he spoke, until her brow touched the front of his shirt. His hand had slid up to cup the underside of her breast and his touch was gentle and bore no trace of urgency. "I'll watch you feed this baby . . . and I'll help you take care of it," he said, his voice deepening with a hint of emotion that surprised her.

His hands had gripped her shoulders as she lifted her head, hardly aware of the silent tears that fell from her glistening eyes.

"Oh, Les . . . I've needed someone to take care of me, to care about me." A sob caught in her throat as she felt the cleansing of her tears, washing away the fears and worry that had tormented her for months. "You really want to marry me?"

Now she turned to him once more, and lifted her face, inviting his caress. "I want to talk to Sara about last night, Les. About staying here with you." Her head ducked against his chest and she leaned for a moment against the solid warmth. "I don't know why I feel a need to make explanations to Sara . . . it's like I want her to know that I'm not playing games . . .''

She looked up quickly and he bent closer. With a familiar gesture that warmed him, she touched his face with her fingertips and then accepted his lips as they brushed against hers. Les felt the smile that formed against his mouth as Marcie spoke in a confiding whisper.

"I expect that Sara is busy defending me to Bess this morning as it is." Her smile became a chuckle. "Bess doesn't really approve of me, you know."

Les's arms circled her waist and he snuggled her against him. "You don't need anyone's approval, but mine, girl."

"I know it," she said. "And you have no idea how good that makes me feel." His hands flexed against her curves, sliding to hold her hips against his body. She shifted invitingly, and he tightened his grip, his long fingers holding her firmly in place.

"Hold it, Marcie girl." His warning chuckle brought her head up in surprise. "I can't keep things under control here if you don't help me. Believe me, there's nothing I'd rather do than take you to my bed and give you the loving you deserve, but that isn't going to happen yet."

She reacted slowly and her hesitation did little to mask the uncertainty that flooded her. "I think I understand, Les. I know you'll probably want to wait until after the baby is born. I realize I'm not every man's idea of . . .''

"Hush!" The quiet command left her with her words unspoken and he covered her mouth with his fingertips. "I'm only willing to wait as long as it takes to get a license and set a date. Next Saturday is about my limit, in fact. After that you can plan on finding out what my ideas are when it comes to you." A grim smile twisted his lips. "Just don't make it difficult for me to pull this off, Marcie. I want it to be right between us before I make you my wife. And it isn't going to be easy for me to wait." He bent to place a tender kiss on her mouth, denying himself the pleasure of prolonging the contact. "Help me, sweetheart." He closed his eyes and touched his brow to hers.

She sighed and whispered his name softly, and the words he heard were like a benediction to his soul. "I love you, Les Cochrane . . . I love you."

TWELVE

News of the upcoming wedding fell like a beneficent blessing upon the soul of Sara Hyatt. Her tender heart had ached for Marcie's unhappiness. Her maternal instincts had been aroused at the thought of Marcie's child entering the world without the presence of a father to welcome it. And her own quiet contentment within the sphere of Cal's presence had only served to make her yearn for an equal share of happiness for her friend.

And now, in the joy that shone from the faces of Les and Marcie, Sara caught the overflow and was happily awash in the excitement of planning a wedding. That it was to be small and select was of no matter. The principals involved really needed no others present. But the requirement of witnesses had brought Cal and Sara into the charmed circle. And so it was that the four of them stood in the small foyer of the Methodist church on Saturday morning.

They were subdued and solemn—Sara, dewy-eyed as she recalled her own hurried wedding, just months ago; Cal, impatient. He tugged at the tie he had been persuaded to wear and watched his wife with well-guarded tenderness. It had occurred to him just moments ago that she was lovelier now than she had ever been and he repressed a smile as he quietly handed her his clean handkerchief. She smiled at him, accepting his offering, and wiped carefully at her eyes, conscious of the grin Cal was holding in check.

Lost in a haze of happiness that permitted no intrusion, Les and Marcie whispered quietly as they stood in the entrance to the small chapel and waited for the pastor to make his appearance.

The service was short and simple. The participants were eager for its completion and only minutes after the first vows had been spoken, the kindly pastor spoke words of blessing and benediction as he sent them on their way.

"I'm really married!" Marcie's first words upon stepping into the sunshine on the steps of the church were followed by a chuckle of delight from her husband.

"Don't laugh at me, Les," she scolded. "I honestly never thought this day would come."

"Well, I'm glad it did, girl," he said as he offered her his arm. "Here, take hold of me. I don't want you falling down these steps."

"I'm probably the clumsiest bride ever married here," Marcie muttered as she clung to him.

"Well, you're my clumsy bride and that's all that matters," Les said decisively. He led her to the car at the curb and helped her get settled in the front seat, then turned to speak to Sara and Cal.

"Thanks for everything. I don't mean to be unfriendly, but Marcie and I have some things to take care of. We'll see ya'll later." With a quick salute, he cocked the ever-present Stetson on his head and dove into the driver's seat of the dusty Chevrolet.

"Well, that was short and sweet!" Sara pouted.

A gruff laugh from Cal and a squeeze of the arm that was draped with familiar ease about her waist brought a quizzical grin to her face.

"What's so funny?" she asked warily.

"You are, sweetheart." He looked down at her and chuckled. "Let's go home and I'll explain it to you, in detail."

The weeks after Thanksgiving passed in a flurry of activity. Sara bent for long hours over the sewing machine, closely guarding her projects from Cal and Bess as she completed gifts for both of them. She planned elaborate menus for their Christmas dinner and discarded them daily as she revised her plans for the holiday. Her moods fluctuated between euphoria and sudden despair as she contemplated the unfinished work to be done in the next weeks.

Cal observed her from afar, seeing a new side of Sara that intrigued him. He constantly became more aware that his wife was more complex than he had first thought. Her talents were many, her moods were becoming changeable, even her looks had undergone a change that he wondered at.

The soft, girlish countenance had become firmed up. The woman who looked at him from glowing green eyes was no longer the youthful creature he had borne here from the low country of South Carolina just months ago. She had matured and developed into a vision of femininity that had brought new dimension to his life.

The doubts that still occasionally assailed him were troublesome, sometimes bringing up a vision of Lou-Ann—a vision he squelched quickly. Much to his surprise, Cal had to admit that all women were not alike. Particularly Sara, as she compared to the other women

he had known. Almost, he could trust her. Almost. But
the knowledge that she held secret a part of her past
nagged at him. Too proud to ask, too unwilling to admit
that it bothered him, he worked at ignoring it.

He worked for long hours after dark in his woodshop,
in the back of the barn. Sara's Christmas gift would be
a wall arrangement for their bedroom. The shelves were
finished, the frames he was attempting weren't. She
had brought a small collection of prints with her, matted
and ready to frame. Pictures of the area in which she
had been born and raised, and Cal knew it would please
her to have them framed and ready to hang where she
could enjoy them.

Bess cooked and baked and daily thanked the heav-
ens for relieving her of Marcie's presence. Things were
back to normal, she decided, and she wanted to keep
them that way. Christmas should be a peaceful, happy
time of year. And so in accordance with Bess's holiday
spirit, the music that filled the ranch house was accompanied by her slightly off-key renditions of familiar
carols.

"Do you think Cal will like this?" Sara held up the
shirt she was finished with and cocked her head as she
inspected the snaps she had just attached. The seams
were finished by hand, with tiny stitches that had taken
more than a little patience to complete. The tails were
extra long so that they would not pull out of Cal's jeans
and the final pressing had been done.

"You know he will, missus," Bess said, agreeing
with a nod of her head. "Right now, he'd like about
anything you do."

Sara flushed and turned away to put the shirt on a
hanger. "I don't know about that, Bess. He didn't like
the tree I picked out for the living room."

"Well, do you blame him? It takes up half the room

and he had to cut two feet off to get it in the house.''
Bess had been secretly pleased by the pseudo-argument
that Cal had indulged in as he and Sara had hassled
over the pine she had chosen and brought home from
town. It had hung four feet over the back of the pickup
truck and took two men to unload it. Only the vision
of her rosy cheeks and sparkling eyes as she scurried
around, giving orders and calling for Bess to come and
see it had saved the day for her.

He could not ruin her pleasure and by the time she
had run to him and hugged him with spontaneous enthusiasm, the battle was won. He had grumbled as he
located the saw. He had sighed deeply as he built a
new tree stand, the old one not being large enough to
hold the stump. And he had complained loudly that
they would be using enough electricity to run a small
city as he strung the lights around the tree after they
had it in place.

Sara had trotted behind him, holding spare bulbs,
offering advice and soothing his temper. Until she
caught the grin he tried in vain to conceal. The evening
had ended with a romp on the carpet that sent Bess to
bed, where she played the television loudly, until she
heard them chase each other up the stairs to their
bedroom.

But the chilly weather that descended in mid-January
gave Sara a new burden to carry. Marcie caught a cold
and Sara made daily trips next door to help out. She
tried to keep Marcie in bed. She cooked and cleaned
and kept Marcie company. And she worried.

Finally, she persuaded Marcie that her simple cold
was in need of a doctor's care. A late-afternoon ap-
pointment was all that was available, but Sara insisted
and Marcie gave in.

With an extra handful of tissues stuffed in her purse

and a new magazine to read, Marcie set off for the doctor's office.

It was time for the boys to come home from school, Les was not expected back at the house for a couple of hours, and Sara faced a dilemma. Cal wanted her home when he got there for dinner. Old-fashioned, maybe . . . but then, he didn't ask for much.

She dialed the phone. "Bess? This is me," she began, knowing that Bess would not be pleased with the news. "I won't be home for a while. Marcie went to the doctor and they're going to fit her in. You know what that means." She chewed her lip and twisted the phone cord. "Look, Bess, tell Cal that I'll cook for Les and the boys and then I'll be home. Go on and have dinner without me."

The phone was silent and then she heard a sigh that needed no words. But Bess was not one to remain silent for long. "Look, missus. Mr. Cal isn't going to like this. I'll tell him, but he'll not be happy about it."

"I know, but I can't help it. Marcie needs me . . ."

"They got along all right before they had either you or Marcie there," Bess announced gruffly. And then ashamed of her bad humor she acceded grudgingly, "But I suspect they could use a hot meal tonight. It's getting colder."

"Thanks, Bess." Sara heaved her own sigh. "Just let Cal know where I am. I won't be late."

"She's not coming home for dinner?" The snarl was more menacing than his booming bursts of temper had ever been, thought Bess. She felt compelled to retreat, even as she realized that Cal's anger was not directed at her, but at the absence of his wife.

She tried for patience and her voice was soothing. "Those boys are all alone, Cal. She said she'd be home as soon as Mr. Cochrane came home or Marcie got back from the doctor.'' One glance at his lowered brows told her that she had failed in her efforts to soothe him.

She had warned Sara, even while knowing that the girl would obey her softer instincts. Cal had an intolerant attitude toward the neighbor. It had gone back too far in the past to disappear this quickly. Had Cal been a tolerant husband, had Les been any other neighbor, the results might not be so predictable.

Bess shrugged her shoulders in a show of nonchalance. "She won't be long now, Cal. It's hardly dark out." She finished setting the table and turned back to him. Dinner was a late affair and the men waited impatiently for her to call them in. But the tension in her kitchen made her hesitate.

Cal broke the short silence. "Feed the men, Bess, and have them close everything down. It's going to rain.''

The scowl he wore was sufficient to waylay any questions as he threw the screen door open and took the porch steps in one long stride. It was almost two hundred feet to the barn where his pickup truck sat, still half loaded with bales of hay that were to be transported to the horses stabled within. He wrenched the door open and with one motion slid onto the seat and plunged the key into the ignition.

Three pairs of eyes watched from the porch and Bess stood in silent worry at the window as the truck lurched in a semi-circle before it hurtled down the long lane to the backtop road.

"Miss Sara's stayed at the Cochrane place to fix dinner,'' Bess explained shortly as the hands filed into the kitchen. Nothing else needed to be said. The whole countryside knew how Cal had felt about his neighbor for years—these men were no exception. They were loyal to Cal, approached idolatry when it came to Sara, and all were aware of the possessive streak in Callen Hyatt when it came to his wife.

"Think we'd better eat and git . . ." The observation was regarded sagely by Bess and she nodded quiet agreement as she placed steaming bowls of food on the table.

"Jay, if your homework is finished, you'd better take your bath and be ready for bed when your dad gets home. You, too, Ronnie." Sara wiped at a stray lock of hair that had persisted in falling across her forehead all afternoon. The dragging sensation across her back told her she was just about at the end of her physical rope for the day.

She wiped the last crumbs from the boys' dinner from the kitchen table. Their childish wrangling could be heard faintly from the bathroom down the hallway and her smile was wistful as she felt a sudden sense of *deja vu*, remembering her brothers as they squabbled over bathroom privileges in their younger days.

A last look around the kitchen satisfied her. Les's dinner waited in the oven and Marcie probably wouldn't even be hungry by the time she got home. A call from the doctor's office had alerted Sara that the wait would be long. Marcie had been sent to the clinic at the hospital for some blood work and Sara had no illusions about the hurry-up-and-wait theories that usually applied in those places.

She poured a cup of the tea that had been brewed an hour earlier and breathed in the strong fragrance. Sitting on the oven vent had kept it hot and she sighed thankfully as she eased into a chair at the table, ready to relax and enjoy its flavor. The night was redolent with the scent of rain in the air and she inhaled the promise of showers to come as she settled her shoulders wearily against the high back of the wooden chair. Only the subdued light from the hallway and the occasional rise and fall of boyish chatter marred the quiet darkness in the kitchen.

"I wonder if Bess got everyone taken care of? I hope Cal doesn't mind that I'm so late." Her softly whispered thoughts made her smile in the stillness of the approaching storm. I sound like a mother hen. The thought amused her and her lips curved in a smile of contentment.

Cal would be waiting for her. Perhaps by the time she returned he would have completed his paperwork for the evening. Her eyes were tender as she contemplated the night ahead.

Rainy, dark hours held secret memories that she cherished. The hurt of her wedding had been thrust into limbo, Cal's disappointment in her had been almost forgotten. She concentrated now on his tenderness, his patience, and the warmth of his embrace that held her so securely. "We've been closer lately than ever before," she decided with a satisfied smile.

Her yawn was unexpected and she felt her eyelids grow heavy. The cup of tea that she held was cooling and her final sip was swallowed with a slight grimace. She wrinkled her nose at the taste. Lukewarm tea was terrible, she thought. The cup was settled in the center of the table and she dropped her head to rest for a moment on her folded arms.

The two little boys that stood in the kitchen doorway a few minutes later crept away quietly after only seconds of silent discussion, their shrugs and stifled giggles deciding the matter. They slipped with stealthy tiptoed footsteps down the hallway, intent on one of their favorite games and the bedroom door shut with hardly a sound behind them.

"Do you think we better go to bed?" The younger of the two was six years old, blond, and round-cheeked, with the softness of his babyhood still upon him.

"Don't be dumb!" Jay stuck out his lower lip with the belligerence of an older brother. His skinny long legs held the promise of height that would equal that of his father and his childish grin was already a carbon copy of the smile that touched his father's mouth on occasion. Showing his authority was a necessity, he had decided long ago. It helped keep his younger brother in line, and he was already aware of the hero worship that lit Ronnie's eyes when he watched him.

He reached out and tumbled the smaller boy into his bed. "Just lay under the covers and I'll leave the light on. We can read till Dad gets home." He tossed a comic book that promised lurid adventure onto the lower bunk and switched off the ceiling light. As he passed the desk, he turned on a smaller lamp that illuminated the room sufficiently for their reading, and then climbed up the end of the heavy maple bedframe, disdaining the ladder that was attached to the side rails.

"Will we get in trouble, Jay?" His reedy voice was worried as Ronnie lay on his back, head over the edge of the mattress, seeking to catch a glimpse of his brother on the top bunk.

"Naw . . . when he comes in, just close your eyes and drop the comic book down on the floor. He'll think we've been asleep for a long time and just turn out the light."

Long practice had perfected his technique and he settled down for a few stolen minutes of intergalactic horror, blissfully unaware that his tactics were well known to his father, tolerated by a generous heart that cherished his two sons.

The quiet approach of the tall rancher scarcely aroused Sara and she was only aware of his presence crouching beside her chair as he gently touched her shoulder.

"Sara?" His fingers brushed against her blouse and he felt her sudden tension under his hand.

"It's Les, Sara," he reassured her.

She tilted her head and her eyes narrowed in the half-light and then he smiled as she recognized him.

"I forgot where I was for a minute, Les. I must have dozed off." She covered her mouth quickly as her breath caught in a yawn. "I didn't realize I was so sleepy." His eyes were amused as she ducked her head. "Some babysitter, aren't I?"

Les watched her quietly as she composed herself and he squeezed her arm gently before he moved his hand to rest on his knee. "I got home as soon as I could, Sara." He looked past her into the hallway. "Where is Marcie? Did she go to bed early?"

Sara shook her head quickly. "I persuaded her to go to the doctor late this afternoon and she had to wait forever to get in. Then he wanted some tests run . . . just precautionary stuff," she hastened to add as she caught sight of his worried expression. "She's stuck in the clinic, but she should be home soon. They close at eight and it's almost that now."

He sighed softly. "I'd forgotten what it was like to worry about a wife, Sara." His grin was crooked and he looked relieved at her explanation.

Her hand reached to touch his arm. "I didn't mind filling in for her, Les. Don't worry, she'll be fine in no time. She just needed to get some medication instead

192 / CAROLYN DAVIDSON

of fighting this off by herself. She'll feel better in a day or so, I'm sure.''

He nodded his agreement. "Probably so . . . and Sara . . . thanks for everything.'' His eyes spoke volumes in the dimness and he watched her with sharp intensity, noting the faint shadows under her eyes, the tired slump of her shoulders, and the weary set of her smile.

"Sara, are you all right? I mean, are you feeling well yourself?'' He spoke in a gentle, caring manner that was at odds with the rough, brusk image he usually presented and she responded with a quiet sigh that told him of her weariness.

"Umm . . . I'm all right, Les. Just tired lately.'' She rubbed distractedly at her forehead and he chuckled softly. Her head swung toward him in surprise and her eyes opened widely as he met her questioning look.

She was so young, so vulnerable, so innocent. He thought she would still retain that elusive quality of freshness even when she reached old age. His fingers touched briefly against her cheek and his smile was tender and knowing.

"Is there a reason, Sara? Are you keeping secrets?'' He laughed softly at her puzzled look and shook his head. "Never mind, little girl. You'll know soon enough.''

"What will she know, Cochrane?'' The low, angry growl spun him into action and he rose from his position beside Sara's chair in a swift motion to face Cal as he entered the back door. The menacing approach of the younger man told Les that Sara's presence in his house was not with Cal's full approval and he stepped back from the young woman who sat in stunned silence between the two men.

"Hyatt.'' Les hesitated a moment, not wanting to

cause a rift in the careful truce that had been established between the two households. With two long steps, Cal shattered that truce as he hauled Sara unceremoniously from her chair, his hands rough against her skin as he jerked her body against his side.

"What will she know, Cochrane?" The question was repeated in a deceptively soft voice and Cal continued without giving the other man a pause in which to reply.

"What are you going to tell my wife? Do you have plans for her, too? Isn't one woman enough for you?"

"Cal!" Her cry was soft, her tones broken with emotion as Sara stiffened against him, but his arm had circled her waist and he gave her no leeway, tightening his grip until she gasped with the sudden pain of his fingers pressed into her waistline.

"Cal, stop this!" She felt a frantic urge to step between the harsh emotions that surged from one man to the other, seeking to absorb the anger that Cal directed at the silent opponent who faced him.

"You don't know what you're saying, Cal. Please don't do this." She begged him without shame, with eyes that threatened to overflow with tears and with an urgency that reached his anger and tempered it for a moment.

He glared with menacing promise at Les before he spun toward the door, half lifting Sara from her feet as she stumbled next to him.

"I'll be back, Cochrane." The words were a promise as he slammed through the doorway and he hesitated only long enough to pull Sara into place in front of him, bending to lift her into his arms.

His long steps carried them down the driveway to where he had left his truck and she closed her eyes and rested her head against his chest, silently thankful that he had not erupted in a volcano of violence.

He dumped her to stand on her feet and then after opening the truck door, he stuffed her with ungentle hands onto the seat. The door slammed, echoing in the stillness of the night and in seconds the pickup truck was rattling through the darkness on the return trip to the Hyatt ranch.

The fury that drove him was totally out of proportion to the circumstances. Even as he felt the waves of anger sweep over him, Cal was aware that he had acted without due cause. He cast a glance at Sara, huddled closely against the passenger door. Her face was averted and only the soft curve of her profile was visible to him.

Silently, he cursed the man who had touched her face, whose hands had been on her skin. He reached across the seat and tugged at her arm, catching her off-guard and she fell toward him with a soft cry of surprise. Her fingers pried at his hand and she twisted her arm beneath his grip.

"Let me go, Cal. Take your hand off me." With no warning, Sara felt the anger flare that she took such pride in controlling. The Black Irish blood that was a legacy from her father carried genes that had given her a temperament she found it hard to cope with. The temper tantrums of her childhood had resulted in shamefaced apologies and tears of regret and by the time she reached her teen years, Sara had taught herself to control the rising anger and found that soft words and gentle behavior brought her the desired results without allowing the release of her wrath upon her family.

The rein she put upon her emotions had become a part of her, but the scene in Les's kitchen had touched off an almost forgotten response. Now, Cal had sparked that response again with his harsh handling of her.

"I said, let go of me, Cal." She spit the words at him and her wrath flared, kindled by his grip on her.

In the darkness, he felt her glare and a short taunting laugh was her answer.

The truck bounced to a halt at the side of the narrow lane, halfway up to the house, and he reached to turn off the headlights before he turned to her. His fingers were like steel against her skin and he smiled with a chill grimace that brought her chin up in defiance. Lifting her, turning her, handling her with an ease that infuriated her even more, he laid her on the long bench seat and levered his body over hers. The long, supple fingers of his left hand feathered over her cheek.

"Does that feel as good as the petting you got from Les?" His voice was deceptively soft, barely whispering between his teeth. She twisted her head away, but it met the back of the seat and she cried out in frustration.

"Damn you, Cal!" She squeezed her eyes shut against the hot tears that threatened to fall. "You have no right to say that." She caught a deep shuddering breath and he brought his fingers to her mouth, touching her lips with arrogant possession.

"Did I arrive too soon for him to taste this?" Even as he spoke he knew the words were hateful and uncalled for, but a need to stamp her with his brand drove him.

"No!" Her muffled cry breathed against the calloused fingertips and to his surprise she bit at him, nipping painfully before he snatched his hand back. She twisted again and the rapid rise and fall of her breasts beneath his arm drew his attention. In the moonlight that fell through the windshield, he watched as his hand lowered slowly across her throat, brushing within the open collar of her blouse, gently, carefully releasing the buttons that kept him from the feminine curves that drew him.

"Stop it, Cal. Let me up . . . don't do this . . ."

She grasped a handful of his shirt and pulled, even as she realized that her strength was futile against his weight. She felt the front of her bra give way under his agile fingers and then his head lowered until his mouth made contact with the rise of her breast, his lips opening to coax her flesh, his tongue working a trail to the crest that even now was peaking in the chill of the night air.

He felt a need for her . . . felt it growing, his anger feeding it, her resistance nourishing it and even as he heard her protests, another voice within him urged him on. His hands gentled, became coaxing, finding and fitting themselves to her curves and hollows.

He forgot everything but Sara, her scent, her warmth and beauty. The place was unimportant, the circumstances were forgotten for the moment. Only the softness of her, the fragrance of her body and the unceasing hunger for her drove him now. Impatient with the barriers of clothing that kept him from her, his hand lowered to the front of her jeans and with ease, he undid the snap and lowered the zipper, lifting from her as he manipulated the denim fabric.

Sara felt a sense of freedom as his body shifted, the weight of him rising, his finger intent on her clothing and she knew his mind and thoughts were focused on possessing her. A cry of denial burst against his shoulder as she tried to shift away from him, struggling desperately against his greater strength.

"No, Cal . . . not like this!" But the battle was over, lost before it really began and she closed her eyes in anguish.

"Please, Cal . . . don't." Her whispered pleas vibrated within her head. She heard them echoing, repeating themselves in a monotonous litany.

Like a vision become reality, the suppressed memory

of another night, another time and place washed over her, and the man who held her took on the form of another. Her cry became frantic as the almost-forgotten, hideous fear of that night became a reality and the bitterness of bile gathered in her throat. The cry became a whimper of distress that spoke of her helpless fear.

"No . . . don't hurt me. Please, don't hurt me . . . please!"

His head lifted, his eyes focused on hers and Cal felt a shame that cleansed his anger and chased the fury from his soul. Sara's face was twisted into a mask of hopeless terror, her lips quivering, her eyes unseeing as small, panting breaths escaped between her lips, whispering words that were broken and pleading.

"Sara, look at me . . . my God, Sara." Incredible remorse flooded through him, washing every vestige of passion before it. She lay helpless beneath him and he cried out in an anguish that matched her own as he fastened her clothing with rough, hasty movements and then lifted her to rest in his arms. He straightened to hold her against him, easing her body until it lay across his chest while he brushed the tendrils of hair from her face. Whispers intended to soothe her fears poured in an unending stream from his lips and he bent to hold his cheek next to hers, swaying back and forth as he rocked her gently.

"I swear to you, Sara. I wouldn't have hurt you, I couldn't hurt you that way. Please look at me, answer me."

As if she had grasped the message his words conveyed, as if she traveled from another place, she opened her eyes and the past became the present.

Cal held her, his anger gone, his arms warm and loving, his voice pleading with her.

"I know, Cal. It's all right . . . I'm all right." She

closed her eyes, needing to sort out her memories from the reality of their conflict. Needing to once more tuck away the hurt of her past, into the secret place where it had been lying, almost forgotten.

"Here, sweetheart. Sit next to me." With gentle hands, he moved her to the center of the seat, his arm still supporting her weight. Then, holding her against him, he maneuvered the truck toward the house, driving in the moonlight, making a slow, careful path as if he feared to disturb her quiet stillness.

The house was silent, only a light over the stove lit the kitchen. Bess, in her room, heard the back door close behind them and she breathed a sigh of relief as the creaking of the stairway told of their passage up the steps.

Sara must have kept things under control, she thought with satisfaction. Otherwise, Cal would still have been fuming. She silently saluted the ability of Sara to handle her husband and settled down once more before the television set, able now to be engrossed in the perils of Doris Day as she scampered through Paris and London in search of her son.

Without turning on a light, Cal led Sara to the bed and sat her on the edge, kneeling before her to slip the shoes from her. She touched his hair as he bent over, carefully pulling her socks off and tucking them into the leather moccasins she had been wearing. He stood, raising her to her feet and gently undid the buttons on her blouse, stilling her silent protest, clasping her hands and kissing the fingers before he released them to fall at her sides.

He slid the blouse from her shoulders and followed it with her bra, his fingers lingering to brush carefully across the fullness of her breasts. She closed her eyes, feeling the rush of pleasure his touch brought, her body once more attuned to his. Her jeans and panties were lowered and she stepped from them, balancing with one hand on his arm.

He reached behind her and pulled back the covers and with gentle caring he lowered her to lie against the cool sheet.

"Cal . . ." She reached for him.

"Shhh . . ." His finger touched her lips and he eased her hands to lie on either side of her head, watching her as he stripped quickly, tossing his clothing aside before he lay next to her.

For long moments the only sounds in the room were those of their breathing as Cal curled her against him, the lean length of his body curved protectively about her own smaller, softer shape. His hands moved slowly over the satin smoothness of her skin, reassuring her, coaxing her without words to nestle against him, giving her the warmth of his presence without demanding any response on her part. He felt the slow melting of her form as she relaxed and snuggled closer, her face turned up into his throat, the fragrance of her breath reaching him as she eased even closer, softening in his arms.

For long minutes they lay quietly, until Sara broke the silence.

"I'm sorry I caused a problem, Cal." The words were not what he had expected to hear. He had glimpsed a new side of Sara tonight. Her anger had made her a stranger to him and he wasn't comfortable with the memory of her wrath. And yet he grudgingly admired the stinging fury she had let loose on him. She had unwittingly exposed a side of herself that had been heretofore hidden.

Secrets . . . what others did she have? His smile was wondering as he thought of the passionate woman she had become as she fought him in the truck, giving him a vision of a fire within her that had been tamped down for too long.

"You didn't cause the problem, Sara. The problem is with me . . . with my jealousy." She felt the tension rise in the hardening of his muscles beneath her fingers and she stiffened in his arms.

"It's all right, Sara. It's something I have to deal with . . . and I'm trying."

"I've never meant to make you jealous," she vowed in a solemn whisper.

"I know that," he admitted. "But the damage was done a long time ago, long before I ever met you." His eyes closed as he offered thanks for the woman he held in his arms. "We'll talk about it . . . soon. I promise."

"Cal, there's something I need to tell you, tonight." The words she had dreaded speaking were suddenly pouring from her and the darkness of the night gave her courage as she began.

"Please, just listen. Don't say anything." She felt his nod as his face moved against her forehead and she drew in a deep breath as if to fortify herself.

"I've never willingly given myself to another man, Cal. For me, you were truly the first, the only man to ever . . ." Her voice trailed off for a moment and she closed her eyes, willing the tremor that gripped her to leave.

"On my graduation night, I went to a party, with a boy I had dated off and on during my whole senior year. He was popular, good looking, and he had always been nice to me, treated me . . . you know, like a friend."

She laughed softly and he strained to hear as her thready tones became strained and almost inaudible. "He drank too much at the party, Cal, and when it was time to leave I should have found another ride. But I didn't. He drove outside of town and I asked him to take me home, but he just laughed and said he wanted to go for a ride, that he wanted to celebrate the biggest night of our lives with me."

She hesitated and a shiver rippled through her as she forced the words that she dreaded to speak. "He stopped the car and began kissing me and pawing at me and I got frightened."

Cal held her closer, as if to shield her from the memories that were flooding her mind. "You don't need to go any further, Sara. I think I know the rest. Just forget it. Hush, sweetheart." He lifted his hand to touch her cheek, brushing at the tears that ran from brimming eyes.

She shook her head abruptly and pushed him back, tipping her face up until their eyes met and she was encouraged as she recognized the quiet understanding in his.

"Let me finish. I've never told anyone, Cal, and I need to say it."

His nod gave unspoken consent and she continued, more slowly, her memories harsh and hurting as she brought them into the open in a final purging that caused pain even as it cleansed and healed.

"He tore my underwear and stockings and pushed me down on the seat. I remember I hit my head on the armrest and my hair got tangled in his fingers. He was heavy and I could hardly breathe. He hurt me, Cal . . . he made me bleed and he left bruises on my legs." She closed her eyes, no longer able to look into his, unable to recite the list of hurts while his face tightened in silent rage.

His fury found words and they were harsh and ragged in her ear as he clutched her against him as if he would take her hurts within himself and protect her from the agony of her past.

"If I had him here . . . if I could get my hands on him . . . I swear to you, Sara, I would kill him for what he's done to you." He shuddered, his big body straining to contain the unvented anger it held.

She laughed softly and it was a bitter sound. "That night, the night it happened, I wanted to die. I prayed to die that night when I got home and I was afraid to tell anyone. My brothers would have killed him and just knowing what happened would have killed my father."

"I wish they had."

"No . . ." she rebuffed his need for revenge with whispered denial. "I couldn't have them hurt, Cal. Don't you understand, I couldn't tell anyone."

She felt his head move in reluctant agreement and she sighed. "I waited a week until my next period. I was so afraid I might be pregnant. I lied to my family and told them I had the flu. I stayed in my room for the first two days and then my father got worried and threatened to call the doctor. So, I had to stage a recovery."

Her laugh was shaky as she shrugged, pushing away from him to watch his face in the dim light. "That's all . . . you know now why I wasn't a virgin on my wedding night. You'll never know how much I wish I had told you before we were married."

Her body sank again into the gentle cage his arms had made for her and she waited quietly while he soothed her with patient tenderness.

Long after she slept, he held her closely until, finally, as the dawn threatened to dispel the final darkness of the night, he closed his eyes and slept fitfully until the sounds of morning activity in the kitchen roused him to face the day.

THIRTEEN

"Cochrane." The voice was low, its tone was crisp, and the man who spoke the single word was behind him.

Les moved his pitchfork unhurriedly, flaking off the hay and tossing it with measured movements until he had given the horse before him its allotment for this morning. His pitchfork was deposited in the bale with an easy motion and he slid his hands into his back pockets before he turned to face Cal. His eyes carefully blank, he nodded in silent greeting and waited for the explosion he was sure would be forthcoming.

Cal shifted uneasily in the wide aisleway, his back to the door that stood open, sunshine streaming past him to reflect on the dust motes that constantly drifted through the air in the barn. This was a trip he had not looked forward to this morning. But his innate pride demanded that he keep his promise to return and his knowledge of Les Cochrane assured him that his neighbor would be expecting him.

"I made a mistake last night." As apologies go, it wasn't a classic, but Les figured, quite accurately, that it was the best he was going to get and his easy grin told Cal that it was accepted.

"I want you to know that I would never do anything to hurt your wife, Hyatt. She's a fine woman and right now she doesn't need any more to occupy her mind than what she already has." He slid a hand from his pocket and lifted it, palm outward, to halt Cal's reply.

"Just a minute, Cal. Let me finish." He waved at the bales of hay that lined one side of the aisle and Cal accepted his unspoken invitation to sit down.

"I don't know if you realize it or not, but I'm crazy about Marcie." He perched on the edge of a bale next to the one that held Cal and his gaze was direct as he continued.

"You know, Marcie kinda had it in mind to move in with me until the baby came, but I couldn't do that. I wanted that baby to have a name . . . and he will, now."

He glanced away and pretended an interest in the cat that had wandered into the open door, leaning down with a studied movement to stroke its back. And then he straightened and rose, his expression somber and his eyes narrowed as if he challenged Cal to dispute his words.

"Look, I'm not going to pretend that I've never noticed Sara or that I couldn't be attracted to her under other circumstances, but this is the way it is. Marcie is what I want and I'm what she needs. We're married now and besides, I'm not one to fool around with another man's wife." It was probably the longest speech Les had ever made, certainly the most eloquent, thought Cal as he tipped his hat back with one finger against the brim.

"Well, somehow that doesn't surprise me, Les. I've never really questioned your integrity." He looked down and tugged absently at a tuft of hay between his knees. His fingers made a production out of selecting a single wisp of hay and he spun it deliberately, watching the twisting fiber. Then with a disgusted grunt he stood abruptly, dropping the green stem to the floor.

"Look . . . I should have known you weren't coming on to Sara. I did know. I just . . . lost it for a minute." His shoulders straightened and he stood erect, his eyes finally meeting those of his neighbor. With a trace of reluctance and a final defiant glare that told Les how difficult this was for Callen Hyatt, he extended his right hand.

"I'd like to forget the whole thing, if you don't mind," he offered.

Without a moment's hesitation, the two men shook hands as they took another step toward mending their fences.

"That's fine with me," Les agreed. "I suspect our women are going to be spending a lot of time together. We might as well figure on getting along with each other."

Cal nodded in silent accord and the men turned, heading toward the wider doorway that faced the ranch house.

"Tell Sara that Marcie is a lot better this morning," Les said as they stood together in the early morning sunshine. "She got home shortly after you left last night. The doctor gave her a shot and some cough medicine and she slept all night."

"Sara will be glad to hear that." Cal privately was delighted that Marcie would be back to tending her own chores, leaving Sara where she belonged.

Les slanted a look at the taller man and rocked back on his boot heels. "You sure shook me up, Hyatt. You know, I thought for a minute there last night that you were going to mop the floor with me. And I didn't want Sara to be involved in something like that." He glanced speculatively at Cal, hesitating a moment before he made a quick, silent decision and continued.

"Maybe I shouldn't say this—but I have a notion I've picked up on something you aren't aware of, Cal."

"What's that?" His head raised and his look was curious and hesitant as Cal stiffened slightly.

Slowly, as if feeling out the atmosphere, Les put his suspicions into words that he hoped wouldn't cause Sara's husband to bristle.

"Your wife makes me think of how my Julie used to look and act when she was first in the family way with the boys." He plunged ahead even as he was aware of the stunned look that washed over Cal's face. "I can't say for sure, but maybe you'll want to keep the idea in mind. It would explain her being tired and looking kinda wiped out these days."

"She hasn't said anything." The words were harsh as Cal frowned in consideration. Sara would surely tell him if she suspected such a thing. Wouldn't she?

"I don't know anything for sure, Hyatt. I just couldn't help but wonder last night. That's what I was talking about when you came in. I hadn't even mentioned it to her. Hell, I had only just gotten home when you saw me squatted down there by her. She'd been dozing at the kitchen table and I'd just woke her up."

He turned fully to face the taller man who looked like he was attempting to digest a new and totally unfamiliar idea. "Head on home, Cal. Talk to her." He nodded toward the house and his grin was eloquent. "I've got a woman in there who's needing a little TLC this morning."

With a two-fingered salute, he turned on his heel and

headed for his back porch, leaving his neighbor to his thoughts.

In a few seconds, his spirits soaring with anticipation, Cal slid onto the seat of his pickup and headed for home.

If Sara was puzzled by the attention she received from her husband during the day, she was even more confused by the questioning looks he cast in her direction whenever he came in the house. Never had he spent so much time on trivial chores that necessitated his presence in and around the kitchen.

"What else do we need from town, Bess?" The pencil was rapidly listing the grocery items she had found on sale in the newspaper ads and the pile of coupons she had cut out were paperclipped together before her as she worked.

Cal watched her from the doorway, a tolerant smile twisting his lips as he noted her concentration. Teasing her was the farthest thing from his mind. Sara's food budgeting was a serious matter and coupon clipping was not a subject for banter, as he had found out early on in their marriage. She was, in this aspect, a determined woman. He had never given her a limit, had encouraged her to buy small luxuries for herself whenever she pleased, but she rigidly held the line and tried never to overspend the allowance she set for herself for the food budget.

Now, he watched as she readied herself for the weekly grocery shopping and with reluctance he stood in the driveway as her car headed for town. He stayed within the area of the house during the afternoon hours and to Sara's surprise, he was waiting for her when she arrived home with the trunk full of brown paper sacks, loaded with a week's supply of foodstuffs.

He sent her to the house with empty arms and her

eyes were puzzled as she looked back to him, bent over
the back bumper, hauling out a double armful to bring
in the house. His careful hovering over her at lunchtime
had been novel. She had luxuriated in his attention and
had even flirted easily with him, much to the amusement of Bess and the three men who watched Cal's
growing frustration at her smiles and touches.

Now, she wondered at his continued attention and
then shrugged briefly as she began putting away the
canned goods and paper products on the shelves in the
pantry. She sensed his reluctance as he made to leave
the house.

"Can I do anything else for you, Sara? Do you need
anything?"

"No." Her tone was wondering. "What is it, Cal?
Is something wrong?"

His smile warmed her and he soothed her easily with
a look. "Nothing's wrong. I'm going out back till dinner time. You take it easy."

The screen door slammed shut behind him and she
stood where he had left her, a faint smile still touching
her lips.

"Dinner will be late, missus," Bess remarked behind
her. "Why don't you go upstairs and take a rest or
read that book you've been wanting to get at all week."
Her suggestion was casual, but her eyes were watchful
as she noted the restrained sigh that Sara breathed.

"Maybe I will . . . I've been trying to find a couple
of hours to read for days."

But the book lay beside her, forgotten as she slept,
when Cal entered their bedroom two hours later. She
lay beneath the comforter, curled on her side with one
small fist beneath her chin, her face flushed in slumber
and her lips parted as she breathed slowly and easily.
Not wanting to rouse her, Cal walked quietly to the

side of the bed and watched her, enjoying the quiet picture she presented. Then, as if she sensed his presence, her eyes opened and without hesitation she smiled, her lips opening to release one small syllable.

"Hi."

"Hi, yourself. I didn't want to wake you." He nudged her aside and she shifted to make room for him as he sat beside her, one long thigh pressed against her hip. His fingers reached with an automatic response and he brushed back the dark curls that framed her face, emphasizing the fragile beauty that had become so familiar to him.

"Bess has dinner ready. Are you hungry?"

She nodded and smiled sleepily as she reached to capture his hand in hers. She read the message in his eyes, that spoke of the hunger he felt and knew that food was not on his mind.

He watched the green eyes that met his and thought of the first time he had seen them—wide in innocence, unknowingly admiring as they fastened upon him, there on the terrace in New York—sparkling gaily at him in the moonlight, as she felt the effects of the punch they shared.

He had felt the desire then, the urgency to be with her, to possess her. His decision to take her home had been automatic, a response to the passion that surged within him. His need to touch her had been immediate and he remembered his impatience with the long cab ride, the elevator that moved so slowly, and the hesitant moments in Marcie's apartment before he had been able to curb his impulse to seduce her.

Even now, he knew that he could have taken her there, on the floor, the couch, or in Marcie's bed. Not for the first time, he was thankful that he had waited, that his good sense had overcome the primitive urge for possession that had driven him that first night. Thankful that her first experience with him had been within the bounds of marriage. She had brought out his protective instincts and once more he was glad that he had been willing to wait for her.

"Cal, what is it? You're looking at me so strangely." She frowned up at him.

"I'm sorry, honey. Nothing's wrong. I was just thinking." His laugh was brief and he tugged the covers from her, pulling her to sit on the edge of the bed.

"Sit still a minute." He left her for a moment and she looked down to find the soft moccasins that were on the floor by the bedside. By the time she slipped her feet into them, he had returned, a warm washcloth in his hand.

"Wipe off your face and hands. It'll help you to wake up." Almost as if he were embarrassed, his voice was gruff and Sara was once more touched by the casually given gestures that spoke of his concern for her.

"Thanks, Cal." Her voice was muffled in the terrycloth and she tossed her head back as she stroked the lines of her throat with the soft fabric before she handed it back to him.

"It will only take a minute to run a comb through my hair and I'll be ready." While he returned to the bathroom, she stood before her dresser and with a few easy movements she had pulled the dark cloud of waves and curls into a semblance of order and fastened a clip in place, leaving a cascade of curls to fall down her back.

He smiled in approval and his hand was warm and possessive on her back as they went to the kitchen, where voices raised in easy banter as the others settled around the big oak table.

As if he were freshly aware of her, Cal paid her

court at the dinner table. The carefully casual touches
of his hands as they passed bowls of food, the pressure
of his thigh against hers as he leaned across to speak
to Bess, and the warmth of his hand as his arm
stretched behind her to clasp her shoulder—all were
gestures that spoke of his possession. By the time the
meal was over, the others were only too aware of the
currents that traveled between them and Sara was
becoming flustered by the attention.

Bess smiled with delight as she began clearing the
table and with a hurried movement, Sara rose to help
her.

"Go do your chores, Cal. I'll give Bess a hand."
As if she were relieved to escape, she slid from her
chair and gathered up dirty plates, turning to the sink
to rinse them off.

Reluctantly, Cal went to the door. "I'll be back
shortly." He cast one last look at her and his eyes
promised that he would keep his word.

But, to his dismay, it was longer than he had planned
and the chores he had hoped to complete rapidly
dragged out as he hauled more hay in the truck and
then helped the men unload it in the barn.

By the time he made his way to their bedroom, Sara
had bathed and was dressed for bed. Propped up on
pillows, she was once more attempting to make inroads
on the book that had been lying next to the bed.

He paused inside the door and his gaze was snagged
by the radiance of the young woman who lay in his
bed. She glanced up at him and her breath caught at
the blatant look of desire that blazed from his eyes.

The golden cast of her skin glowed in the dim light
from the bedside lamp. An inch above the neckline of
her gown, he saw the definite line where summer tan
left off and the creamy rise of her breasts began. His

eyes fastened there and in his mind he undid the buttons and laid the fabric wide to feast on the beauty beneath the soft, clinging batiste.

An awareness of his thoughts brought an answering light of desire to her green eyes and his narrowed in recognition as he watched her reaction.

"Hold that thought, sweetheart." His words were abrupt and she shivered with anticipation as he headed for the bathroom. His fingers made short work of the buckle on his belt and through the open doorway she saw flashes of brown, muscular back and long, tanned arms as he smoothly removed his jeans and underwear. A glimpse of white backside was her last look at him before he stepped into the shower and she slid down into place, waiting for him, knowing that his bathing would be quick and his return to her would be within minutes.

His first flurry of hunger appeased, Cal lifted his head from her slowly, his lips moist from the long kisses they had just shared. His fingers carefully and tenderly dealt with the buttons on her gown as he lived the fantasy he had courted earlier. He was not disappointed. The delicate shape of her breasts was a never-ending source of delight to him.

She laughed softly and he was pleased at her self-conscious pleasure as she watched him. The power she held over him was no longer a threat, it was a shared joy.

Somewhere in the long, dark hours of the night past, he had relinquished the control he had fought so hard to retain. Within her slender fingers she held the secret of his happiness. Unknowingly, she had been setting the pace in their marriage. He had only been shadow boxing, maintaining his distance, even while she drew him ever closer within her web of passion. So easily, she lured him . . . with a smile, a touch, a whisper. So readily, he followed her lead, assuming control when it pleased him, as if to reassure himself that he truly was in charge.

And the paradox of it all was that she was totally unaware of her power. In her softness, she had won his strength, with her loving ways, she had earned his devotion. Because of her honesty she had received his complete trust. And now, he dealt with the question that had baffled him throughout the day. After being so honest with him last night, could she be keeping a secret as important as a pregnancy from him? With a slow shake of his head, he denied it.

His smile was an enigma to her. His behavior had puzzled her all day but she waited with patience, knowing that the newness of their relationship would not be marred by problems now. The freshness of his attitude had been like a breath of spring and she gloried in it. Gone were the momentary lapses that marred their loving, the thoughtful pauses before he left his unhappy thoughts and came back to her.

His lips dropped to caress the rise of her breast, running a line of kisses along the tender, lifting swell that culminated in a rosy crest. She relished the curling, heated flare of desire that penetrated her at his touch. So attuned to his mood, so ready to love him, so eager for the joy he brought her, she waited.

She's all I ever wanted, he thought, as a surge of happiness expanded within him. He captured the emotion that flared into being, anxious to examine it for a moment. His eyes lit with discovery as he rose above her and surprised a languid, heated passion in hers that told him she shared the love he felt.

She could never have surrendered herself to him so readily, so fully, if she did not love him. The half-whispered words in the night that he had tucked into his subconscious bloomed now in the light of his discovery and for the first time, he was able to repeat those words, finally knowing their meaning as he spoke them for the first time.

"I love you, Sara. I didn't realize it before, but I've loved you almost from the start."

A shiver, so small he scarcely noticed it, touched her body. The thrill of his words, the unexpected gift, this expression of his love, brought quick tears to her eyes. She was unable to speak for a moment, and then as he watched, a smile of unspeakable beauty lifted her lips and she closed her eyes, forcing a crystal drop to slide from beneath each eyelid. She laughed, a quivering sound of joy that brought an answering low chuckle from him. Able finally to speak, she whispered, as if she could not trust her voice to respond to her command.

"Oh, Cal! I've loved you for so long. I've wanted to tell you so many times. But I've felt so guilty for not being honest with you, for hurting you with my deceit."

His mouth stopped her and his kiss healed her. She felt the love outpoured as his entreaty soothed her.

"Don't ever let me hear those words from you again, Sara. Promise me, please."

"Yes, all right. Whatever you say." She laughed with delight, her fingers drawing him back to her, clasping her hands behind his neck.

"Sweetheart?" His whisper was low.

"Hmmm . . ." She was busy easing her way between his lips.

"Sweetheart, are you a little late?" Not the most subtle of hints, he thought with amusement.

"Late for what?" Slowly, she was gaining her objective, her tongue busy at the slow job of learning the texture of his lower lip.

"Your period, love." Her eyes flew open and he knew that the puzzled surprise was genuine. And then she smiled in reassurance.

"I've been a little late before, Cal." Her brow knitted in a frown and he saw the concentration as she mentally checked off the days and weeks.

A slow awakening, an awareness of the time involved began to penetrate, and he caught a glimpse of uncertainty in her eyes.

"Cal? I'm really quite sure that I had a period last month. At least I think I did . . ."

She pushed him aside with a strength that surprised him and slid from beneath him with a fluid grace that he admired even as he fell to one side. Sitting up in bed beside him, she frowned again and glanced down at him, as a flush stained her cheeks.

"It's been a while . . . since Thanksgiving." She hesitated and turned her hands up in a gesture of supplication.

"Help me think, Cal." She glared at him suddenly as a grin twitched at the corners of his lips. "This isn't funny!" she cried even as an answering smile lit her face.

"Cal? What do you think?" The breathless, innocently beguiling expression on her face was more than he could hold still for and his arms swept out to catch her, drawing her to lie across his chest.

"Yes, sweet, what is it?" His eyes were amused and he kept his jubilance under control with an effort that tightened his grip on her arms.

"Cal, I'm really late. I mean, really, as in two months late!" She sought his eyes with an eagerness that bordered on fear. "Cal, you don't care? You're not upset about this, are you?"

"Of course I care, you little fool. I care more than you can possibly know." He lifted her higher against him and his mouth laid a trail of moist kisses, pouring out upon her a fountain of love and adoration that far surpassed any she had ever known.

"I was so blind, Sara. I placed so much value on the question of your virtue and it was so unimportant. The qualities I wanted in a wife were right in front of me and I was too blind to see them." He brushed his mouth across her forehead and inhaled her scent, her sweetness.

His lips spoke against her silky flesh and the words were tender. "You are so innocent, my Sara . . . so . . ."

"After all you've taught me? How can you say such a thing!"

He smiled and she felt his lips curve as they touched her cheek. "It's a relative term, love. There is a quality in you that defies definition. Purity comes to mind and yet that word makes you sound pious. I think it's the purity of your motives and the innocence of your giving."

He turned quickly, rolling her beneath him and lowered his head to rest gently against her breast and her fingers twined in the gold of his hair as she held him there. "You put me to shame, Sara. You offered me so much and I gave so little in return." His words were hesitant and she felt the pain in them.

"I gave it all once . . . years ago when I was very young and hadn't learned to choose wisely. She didn't want my love, Sara. She wanted money and position and another man . . . and didn't have the decency to tell me so. I vowed I'd never trust another woman again, and I never had reason to, until you showed up. Even then, I was afraid to love you.'' He lifted his head and his eyes were solemn as they looked into hers.

"It took a while, but I finally realized that you had filled my life with all the sweet, good things I'd always needed. And you filled all the spaces within me that needed loving.'' His fingers took hers and he laced their hands together, his covering and capturing hers within the strength of his grasp.

"Of course, I want our child, Sara. I've never wanted anything more in my life, except you.''

Her murmurs were soft and broken against his chest as she snuggled closer to him. "A baby . . . Oh Cal . . . a baby!'' She pushed him away until she could look once more into his eyes and then her fingers touched his cheeks tentatively.

His face was damp and her look was unbelieving. "Cal? Are those tears?''

"Of course not,'' he denied, even as his smile told her that he lied. "How can anyone as happy as I am right now, possibly cry?''

"Oh, it's easy, Cal. I do it all the time.'' She laughed in delight and her arms tightened, drawing him closer.

Their whispers filled the night and their happiness reached culmination hours later when the inevitable result of their joy brought them together in a loving so tender, so pure, so filled with undiluted pleasure and happiness that it gave new meaning to the love that filled their hearts.

EPILOGUE

"What shall we call her?" Cal's eyes filled with wonder as the wide, slate-colored gaze of his daughter turned toward him at his words. So intent was her look, so like the piercing, knowing intensity of her mother's eyes that he was awed.

She had responded to his voice and her miniature fingers tightened their grip on the index finger they held. A grip that brought a blurring to his vision as he began to grasp the miracle of new life. A blending of Sara and himself, the end result of their love for each other.

"Can we call her . . ."

"How about . . ."

Their words were simultaneous and then they both waited for the other to continue.

"My mother's name was Kathleen," Sara ventured.

Cal's grin was delighted. "My mom was Catherine."

"Why didn't I know your mother's name? I don't think you've ever mentioned it, Cal." Her eyes lighted with pleasure.

"We can just call her Katie."

His hand brushed carefully, tenderly against the dark head that nestled against Sara's breast. The tiny fingers, that had curled so instinctively around his, relaxed as she slept and he traced the length of each with his index finger.

"I thought I wouldn't know how to love a baby," he confessed softly.

"And do you?" she whispered.

"Oh, yes . . . I love her." His lips touched almost hesitantly against the swirling crown of his daughter's head and then he straightened and his eyes met those of his wife.

"I'm not good at this, Sara. I don't have the right words . . . how do I tell you . . . what can I say, so that you'll know how I feel?" He leaned to her, capturing her lips in a kiss that spoke of an emotion he could not find words to express, that speech could never describe.

She reveled in it, in the act of love they shared and her whisper gave him the answer he needed to hear. "You just did, Cal . . . you just did."

SHARE THE FUN . . .
SHARE YOUR NEW-FOUND TREASURE!!

You don't want to let your new books out of your sight? That's okay. Your friends can get their own. Order below.

No. 51 RISKY BUSINESS by Jane Kidwell
Blair goes undercover but finds more than she bargained for with Logan.

No. 52 CAROLINA COMPROMISE by Nancy Knight
Richard falls for Dee and the glorious Old South. Can he have both?

No. 53 GOLDEN GAMBLE by Patrice Lindsey
The stakes are high! Who has the winning hand—Jessie or Bart?

No. 54 DAYDREAMS by Marina Palmieri
Kathy's life is far from a fairy tale. Is Jake her Prince Charming?

No. 55 A FOREVER MAN by Sally Falcon
Max is trouble and Sandi wants no part of him. She *must* resist!

No. 56 A QUESTION OF VIRTUE by Carolyn Davidson
Neither Sara nor Cal can ignore their almost magical attraction.
